JESUS TO JESUS

Jesus to Jesus: *Prophet Isa Returns to Battle the Dajjal, Revised Edition*
Syed Nadim Rizvi - with Jack Snyder and Pamela Cosel

CITRINE PUBLISHING SERVICES, LLC
9810 FM 1960 West #295
Humble, TX 77338

In Association with
Elite Online Publishing
63 East 11400 South Suite #230
Sandy, UT 84070
www.EliteOnlinePublishing.com

Cover design by: Avatardesk | info@avatardesk.com
Printed in the United States of America

ISBN: 978-1-961801-05-9 (eBook)
ISBN: 978-1-961801-04-2 (Paperback)

DEDICATION

I dedicate this book to the promotion of peace and
interfaith harmony in the world.

INTRODUCTION

In the vast tapestry of human history, there have always been tales and prophecies that speak of an ultimate culmination of events—a time when the world as we know it will reach its grand finale. Across cultures and religions, these visions of the end times have captivated the hearts and minds of believers, serving as a reminder of the transient nature of our existence and the inevitable return to the Divine.

While the narrative of the apocalypse has been recounted though various mediums, including literature and film, this book promises a refreshing take, offering a unique perspective on the tale of the end times. Through innovative storytelling and fresh insights, it aims to redefine familiar themes, inviting readers to embark on an enlightening journey unlike any other portrayal of this captivating narrative.

Within these exciting pages you will witness a world teetering on the precipice of chaos, where darkness creeps into every corner, when a prophesied time emerges—a time that has been foretold since ancient scriptures. This is a tale that unravels at the intersection of faith, destiny, and human struggle.

As a foundation for our story, we use the Quran and the sayings of Prophet Muhammad (peace be upon him), which provide detailed descriptions of the events that will transpire before the end of the world, including the appearance of the Antichrist/Dajjal, the return of Jesus/Isa (peace be upon him), and the final confrontation between the two. These prophesied events have been the subject of countless discussions, interpretations, and debates among scholars and laypeople alike.

"Jesus To Jesus: A Tale of the End Times & Interfaith Harmony, Giving Christians & Jews a New Perspective on Christ" is an epic story where we delve into the realm of the eschatological, where the boundaries between the seen and the unseen begin to fade. Within the pages that follow, the ancient prophecies come alive, whispering of portents, signs, and the ultimate reckoning that awaits mankind.

As the world grapples with its own demons, a rising star television journalist named Fatima, a Muslim who's lost her faith, will find herself thrust into extraordinary circumstances as she embarks on a journey that will test all she knows and believes, challenge her understanding of reality, and force her to confront the very essence of her existence.

Along on this journey with her is Ali, her cameraman and devout and knowledgeable Muslim, and Paul, a CIA operative and atheist. Together, the three of them set out to navigate the treacherous landscape of the End Times, where deceptions and trials are plentiful, and where they must confront and deal with their respective beliefs and perceptions.

Amidst it all is Jesus/Isa (peace be upon him) descending from Heaven, the Mahdi, who is the revered Imam prophesied to appear near the End Times, and the Dajjal, an evil figure who has walked the Earth from the dawn of its existence.

This is a story that transcends time and space, immersing readers in a vivid adventure of prophecy, spirituality, and the eternal struggle between good and evil. As we delve deeper into the pages of this book, we may contemplate the nature of our own existence, our purpose in this world, and the choices we make that shape our destiny.

Prepare to embark on a gripping narrative that illuminates a new perspective of the End Times—a tale that merges the spiritual and the earthly, the divine and the human, as we traverse the final chapters of our shared journey. Welcome to a world where faith is tested, hope remains steadfast, and the promise of divine justice flickers as a guiding light in the darkest of times.

May your journey through the pages of this book provide enlightenment, inspire contemplation, and ultimately foster a deeper connection to our Creator as the characters unravel the mysteries of the End Times.

It is my hope that you will not only learn new aspects of eschatology, but enjoy the great adventure experienced by our interesting and endearing protagonists within the pages of this book.

Syed Nadim Rizvi
2023

CHAPTER ONE

"When Jesus was only 12 years old, he asked a rabbi: Isn't God powerful enough to hear our prayers anywhere? Isn't He in our hearts? No matter where we are?" Ali Abrahim said as he and Fatima Al-Hasan rode the elevator to the roof of Herod's Palace.

"This was during Passover in Jerusalem," Ali continued. "This began his life of opposition to the religious authorities of the time. Those present were both shocked and amazed at the knowledge and wisdom this boy possessed."

Fatima Al-Hasan passively listened. She was distracted with their upcoming assignment, which was the most important one for them to date.

"Though Jesus spent most of his time on Earth in Jerusalem, Muhammad was only here near the end of his life," Ali said, "but neither were ever at Herod's Palace according to Islamic teaching."

Ali gathered his thoughts before resuming. "The story of his trip to Jerusalem is amazing and wonderful, though. As

Muhammad slept in the Ka'bah, the sacred shrine of Mecca, the archangels Gabriel and Michael came and purified his heart, then he was carried to Jerusalem by the winged creature of Buraq," Ali said gazing off as if witnessing the events himself. "From there, where the Dome of the Rock would eventually be built, Gabriel took Muhammad to the first heaven and proceeded through all seven levels until they reached the throne of Allah. Along the way he met many prophets including Yahya and Isa."

Ali turned to Fatima in the large elevator. "You know – John and Jesus."

Fatima chuckled, a mix of amusement and annoyance evident in her laughter. "I know the other names for Yahya and Isa, but it's been years since I thought about such things," she admitted, not bothering to meet his gaze as the elevator ascended. Clearly preoccupied, she added, "The Prime Minister should be arriving any minute. I should go over my notes." Retrieving a small notepad and a pencil from her purse, she prepared herself as the elevator came to a stop.

The sun blinded them briefly as they stepped through the doors onto the terrace. Fatima shaded her eyes with a hand as Ali, her cameraman, went to work setting up the gear. He pointed the lens in the general direction of the Dome of the Rock as he tightened the camera onto a tripod. They were quite a pair, looking out of place dressed in American clothing. Both in their mid-twenties, they seemed full of energy and optimism.

Ali looked around at the few benches and various potted plants scattered about, noting that most were in bloom. From this vantage point, the terrace looked pretty much like any other terrace in Jerusalem, not one atop the majestic Herod's Palace. Hence, his reason for framing the breathtaking Dome of the Rock in the shot. It was important to let their audience know exactly where they were. He knew Fatima would approve without discussing it with her.

Fatima took deep breaths as she looked off into the distance at the Dome of the Rock, hands on her hips. "Such history. We are standing on holy ground in a holy place. Prophets. Kings. Martyrs. They've all been through here." She tossed Ali a smile, but he looked lost in thought.

"What's on your mind, Ali?" she asked, taking a step closer to where he stood.

He stared at the Dome of the Rock as if hypnotized. "Standing here in the midst of the Holy Land, I can't stop thinking of something I read last night." He took a deep breath and continued. "'Indeed, from the offspring of this man there shall emerge a folk whose tongues shall be moist from reciting God's Book, but it shall not go past their throats. They shall pass through the religion just as an arrow passes through a hunted game.'"

"That was beautiful, Ali. It sounded like poetry."

"Those are Muhammad's words."

"What do they mean?"

He looked at her with an intensity she hadn't seen from him before. "He was speaking about the Kharijites. They will appear religious and be more constant in their prayers, fasting, and other acts of worship than the rest of the Muslims. They will pay lip service to the faith, but it will just pass right through them. Today we see that in the extremist group called TRIAD, which was originally founded by Muslims, though they have expanded beyond that faith to include extremist Christians, Jews, Hindus, and many other faiths. Even secularists."

Fatima winced as she thought about the terrorist group which had formed within the past year and was responsible for many horrible acts and deaths around the world.

"In the past it was ISIS, Al Qaeda, and many of the mullahs," Ali said. "And in others who kill in the name of religion, such as The Army of God, Phineas Priests, and Covenant, Sword, Arm of The Lord, all of which are Christian terrorist groups. They are all present-day Kharijites. And they are all liars that twist the words of the faiths they claim to follow. TRIAD is a lie within its very name. Truth, Ritual, Intercession, Devotion and Atonement. They are none of these things. But they use this lie to attract new recruits. It's disgusting." He turned his back on the Dome and fiddled with the camera.

"What does Intercession mean in the context of this group?" Fatima asked.

"It's supposed to mean Intercession of the Spirit or Deity, or whatever one believes," Ali explained, looking at her with raised hands. "But in the hands of this group, all the words are meaningless and mean the exact opposite of their intended meaning: Truth is lies, Ritual is discord, Intercession is non-intervention, Atonement is abandonment, and Devotion is disloyalty. This group is composed of true Kharijites in every possible way. They are the worst of the worst."

Fatima quietly pondered Ali's words as she gazed out over Jerusalem. *Such a rich past with all three Abrahamic faiths. And yet, so much violence spanning its history. Will it ever come to an end? And if so, how? It seems like it will take nothing short of a miracle to accomplish it.*

Together they stood and took in the stunning view of the ancient buildings and rolling hills. A stillness fell over them as they became lost in solemn thought. It was so quiet that the sudden opening of the terrace doors startled them.

From the hallway opening, a half-dozen men wearing identical dark suits walked out onto the roof. They quickly spread out, checking the area, looking around every corner.

Ali watched them closely. *This is probably the Shin Bet. And they are most likely armed with automatic weapons, such as AK-47s,* he thought, though he could not see any visible weapons on them.

When the men in suits seemed satisfied all was in order, they faced one man who stood in the center of the roof and nodded to him. He spoke quietly into a microphone mounted on his right sleeve.

A moment later, a tall, handsome man who appeared to be in his mid-fifties, dressed in traditional Israeli clothing and keffiyeh headdress, stepped out onto the roof into the sunlight. It was Israeli Prime Minister Nicholas Wilder. Alongside him was a young, blonde woman, his assistant. Behind them were two men dressed in suits, all of them undoubtably part of his security detail.

Fatima noticed the Prime Minister walked deliberately, with a calm and commanding presence. His salt-and-pepper gray beard was immaculately groomed.

"May I present to you the Israeli Prime Minister, Nicholas Wilder," his assistant said to Fatima and Ali. She moved aside, her demeanor professional as the Prime Minister stepped forward.

"Hello, Miss Al-Hasan. I have been looking forward to meeting you," the Prime Minister said, nodding to her. They exchanged handshakes.

Fatima spoke slowly and with confidence. "Thank you, sir. I have been looking forward to meeting you, also. This is my cameraman, Ali," she said, gesturing with her arm in his direction.

Nicholas glanced from one to the other and warmly smiled. His bodyguards stood a respectful distance away.

"So, are you both of the Muslim faith?"

"I am, sir," Ali proudly replied. He stood a bit taller.

Fatima blushed. "More of an agnostic these days, Mr. Prime Minister."

"Nothing wrong with that, Miss Al-Hasan. Searching is good for the soul."

The Prime Minister turned his attention to Ali. "That is wonderful," he said as he clasped his hands. "Together we are all connected by our father, Abraham." He turned to look out at the city. "It is a lovely view, isn't it?" he said, taking in the sight of the Dome of the Rock. "Our heritage. The seat of our faith, also so very special to the Jews, Christians, and

Muslims. The most special place on Earth, in my opinion. Jerusalem is filled with holy sites important to all our faiths. It is my hope and dream that we can all live in peace alongside each other and pray."

There was a solemn moment of silence after his comment, then Fatima took over the conversation. "We will be ready to go live in just a minute. Please allow us to check with our newsroom staff back in the States."

"Of course," the Prime Minister said as he relaxed and sat down on a bench. The shade of the tree cooled him, for which he was grateful. Ali stepped closer to him and attached a remote microphone to his tunic.

Christopher Munson and the *News World* production team in New York readied at the other end of the transmission. All was on schedule. "Fatima, are you there?" he asked over the microphone. He was a handsome man in his late forties, fit and trim with a glistening smile whose voice conveyed his appealing confidence. The very on-screen image of the network.

Fatima heard his voice loud and clear through her earpiece. "Yes, Christopher, we're here. Ali is ready to roll. Just give us the countdown," she said. She'd already positioned the Prime Minister where he should stand. Behind him, just over his left shoulder, was the Dome of the Rock in the background. She smiled into the lens.

"10, 9, 8, 7..." began the countdown in her earpiece. Ali heard it too, and when the count reached one, he pointed his finger at Fatima and mouthed, "You're on!"

She heard Munson's voice in the earpiece. "…and now we go to Fatima Al-Hasan, our news correspondent reporting from Jerusalem."

Fatima saw in the monitor positioned next to Ali that the image had switched from Munson to her. "Thank you, Christopher. I'm here on top of the Tower of David site, also connected to the ancient Herod's Palace. With me is Israeli Prime Minister Nicholas Wilder."

The camera lens panned from Fatima to include a wider shot of the Prime Minister, smiling, as the angle also took in a view of the background scene. The cityscape showed viewers the breadth of the location from which they talked. There was not a cloud in the sky.

"Thank you for joining us, Mr. Prime Minister. It is an honor to be talking with you."

"Thank you, Miss Al-Hasan."

"This is an interesting location you have chosen for the interview," Fatima said, anticipating his reply to explain the area's history.

"Yes," he nodded. "Herod Antipas as well as his father, King Herod, was a powerful man back in his day. Now his palace is part of the Tower of David Museum and is becoming a major tourist site." He hesitated a moment, and Fatima remained silent. "But the reason I chose this location is because of the mosque which you see behind us near the Dome of the Rock." He gestured toward the building.

Fatima heard production chatter in her ear. "Tighter on the mosque." Fatima saw on the monitor that the view of the dome filled the screen. Ali was doing a great job, as usual.

The Prime Minister continued, "The Al-Aqsa Mosque. Third holiest site for the Islamic religion on the entire planet. Closed off to all visitors, except Muslims. In some ways, this is symbolic of the strife in the region." He stared straight into the lens, his next words louder and firm. "We have too much division and separation among all Christians, Jews, and Muslims. It is my goal to end the centuries-long conflict in the Middle East!"

Fatima was surprised and did not hold back on her questioning. "With all due respect, Mr. Prime Minister, there are those who would say that is just a pipe dream. Not possible in this day and age."

The Prime Minister laughed, but it wasn't one of condescension or arrogance. It was joyous. He was happy to get into a deep discussion on the matter.

Bright sunlight reflected off the golden surface of the Dome of the Rock as security guards and Israeli soldiers patrolled the grounds below the live interview site. They kept a watchful eye on a parade of visitors who walked about, taking pictures, enjoying the day.

Two Muslim women, dressed in niqabs, walked side-by-side with a group of Muslims toward the Al Aqsa Mosque. Their eyes were hidden in the shadows of their clothing.

As they approached the Dome of the Rock, one of the women veered off from the group and headed for the dome.

The other one continued to tag along at the end of the group. The guards and soldiers ignored them. They were just more Muslims visiting to pray. This was a common activity every day, and it flew beneath the radar of what should be noted. But had the guards paid closer attention, they would have seen these two women were not really part of any group attending today.

The ancient mosque had been through a lot in its rich history – multiple empires, periodic earthquakes, and repairs and reconstruction over the centuries. Many challenges. And it was about to face another challenge.

The group disappeared into the mosque to pray. But not the woman who entered with them. She had other plans.

On the roof of the palace, the Prime Minister was in his element, as public speaking came naturally to him. "Peace is definitely attainable," he said. "And in our time. You just have to want it badly enough. Haven't so many suffered from the atrocities of bombings and shootings? Even in the United States – supposedly a safe country – there are those who kill others because of religious beliefs or cultural background differences. When will it stop? We, today, must do something now! Mankind has had enough hatred, enough spilled blood!" At that last remark, he pounded a fist into the opposite hand.

With that comment, back in the New York newsroom, Munson yawned and wondered where this interview was going. In a whispered voice, he spoke to Fatima. "Miss Al-Hasan, we need to pick up the pace of this interview. He's not saying anything that is worth noting to this point." Christopher watched Fatima subtly nod on his monitor, half a world away.

"Sir, that is a very ambitious goal, to have peace in the Middle East. How do you expect to accomplish that?" she asked.

Christopher smiled. *Good. A direct question that requires a direct answer. A successful interview requires the subject be put on the spot.*

The interior of the Al Aqsa Mosque was more than beautiful, it was breathtaking. Huge with red-and-white tiles, marble pillars, and arches. Shafts of sunlight shone down through large windows as if from Heaven itself. The air carried a sweet fragrance better than the most expensive perfume.

Muslims of all ages knelt and prayed. The group that the woman had followed in spread out and joined the Muslims who were already inside. Except for the woman. Lingering behind the others, she kept her head down and disappeared behind a wide column. Making sure no one was looking; she broke off and made her way down a secluded corridor.

Back at the newsroom, Munson checked with the production staff and affirmed that millions were watching the interview around the world, in living rooms, bars, campus dorm rooms, on mobile devices, and in classrooms. "Just what we hoped for," he said to himself. Munson turned his attention back to the interview.

"Most governments claim they base their decisions on economics, whereas in reality, everything is a simple policy decision," the Prime Minister said. "Countries that claim they cannot afford their entitlement programs, or education, or infrastructure, seem to have a never-ending budget for war. My goal is to steer spending away from conflict and put it into making Israel an equitable place for all its citizens and residents. I believe this will open up peace talks between the three Abrahamic religions – Christianity, Judaism, and Islam. If people are treated with respect, as equals, they will be more willing to come to the negotiating table and share ideas." The passion in his voice was clear.

Munson laughed and touched the communication switch to Fatima's earpiece. "He is starting to sound a bit crazy, isn't he?" he said to her. A few nearby technicians chuckled.

On the monitor, Fatima subtly glanced toward the camera and gave a weak smile, knowing he could see her expression. She liked Munson but thought he could be too much at times.

The Muslim woman hurried down the empty stone-and-marble hallway, being as stealthy as she could to avoid as much echo as possible. She slowed and pressed her back against a wall, looking both ways. She reached up, touched her ear, and mumbled something. Then hesitated as if listening. After a moment, she continued down the hallway. No one followed her.

Six thousand miles away in New York City, a technician in the *News World* control room scrunched his face with concern. He spoke into Munson's earpiece.

"Sir, I'm picking up a slight interference in our audio signal. I don't know what's causing it."

"Okay, figure it out, let's get it fixed," Munson said as he turned to the show's director while he was off-camera.

Ali turned the lens from the direction of the Prime Minister to show more of the background scene. He whispered in his mouthpiece, "Fatima, keep it going. We'll figure out the sound issue."

"Mr. Prime Minister, there are those who do not support your view," Fatima said, proceeding with the interview. "How do you plan to get them on board with your idea of creating peace among all three religions?"

In the isolated corridor of the Al Aqsa Mosque, the Muslim woman whipped off her niqab revealing she was not a woman at all. She was a Caucasian man. Short with a thin frame to pass as a woman more easily, he had bricks of C-4 explosives wrapped around his body. On the left side of his waist, attached to his belt, was a pack of instruments needed to set off the C-4. On his right side hung a sleek Glock 9mm with a silencer secured firmly to his belt with a gun clip.

With expert precision, he pulled the belt of C-4 bricks off his body and quickly pressed blasting caps from his bag into them. He next connected the caps to a detonator, then finished by attaching a timer.

He was placing the belt of C-4 bricks against the base of a support column when an Israeli soldier strolled around the corner. His rubber-soled shoes had kept his movements silent.

The two men stared at each other, not flinching, for a minute before they leaped into action, going for their guns. The bomber was faster and better trained. The Glock came off his belt so swiftly it appeared to not have been in a holster.

Thwip – thwip! Two slugs from the silenced Glock, and the soldier went down. He moaned. *Thwip.* One more in the head stopped his anguished sound.

The man returned to work with the casualness of someone with a desk job. He clipped his gun back onto his belt and spoke into his headset.

"I'm about to set the timer in the mosque," he said.

"Same here in the dome," came the response through his earpiece.

"Okay, let's do it." He quickly pulled off his headset and discarded it to the floor.

He put the niqab back on and set the timer for sixty seconds, then bolted out through a side door. No reason to clean up after himself. In less than a minute the blast would take care of the mess he had made.

"The interference has disappeared," the technician said, hunched over his equipment in the *News World* control room. Munson nodded approval from his anchor desk. He couldn't see that the technician looked troubled. But a nearby production assistant saw it.

"What's wrong?" the production assistant asked.

"I didn't do anything to get rid of it. It just stopped on its own."

"That's good though, right?"

The technician shrugged but was still concerned.

Two Israeli soldiers spotted the man dressed as a Muslim woman running from the mosque. They exchanged perplexed glances, then pursued with one of them shouting, "Ma'am! Ma'am! Hold up! Is there a problem?"

He ignored them as he sprinted toward the security wall.

"Something strange is going on at the dome," a voice said over the guards' radios. One of the guards glanced back and spotted a second niqab-wearing Muslim woman dashing from the Dome of the Rock in the opposite direction.

The Prime Minister looked over at the Dome. "By extending an olive branch to our – assumed – enemies, I hope to create a peaceful exchange. If we don't do that, the problems will reach the point of no return. This is not a problem with a solution lying at the hands of a single person or country, however. Only through collective efforts can we achieve the goal of peace. I am trying to fulfill my responsibility by being the first to take a step forward."

As dozens of Muslims prayed in the mosque, another Israeli guard strolled down the hallway making his rounds. He had no idea that this was the last walk he'd ever take. Or the last thing he'd ever do, for that matter. He stood still and gasped when he came upon his dead colleague lying on the cold marble floor. The dead man's head was turned to the side. Coincidentally, his open eyes stared straight at the C-4 belt. The guard followed his friend's dead gaze right to the explosives. And then to the timer where less than ten seconds remained. The guard stared dumbfounded as the seconds ticked off.

"The entire world is heading for a cliff," Prime Minister Wilder continued, as Fatima and Ali listened intently, along with millions of viewers worldwide. *News World* had affiliate stations across the globe as well as a livestream on their website. "It will end in disaster if we don't do something. A tremendous amount of blood has been shed over many years. Hatred has crept into the world's societies and there remains no more room for destruction."

He faced Fatima, "We must make sincere efforts toward peace and unity."

The guard sighed deeply as the timer on the bomb hit zero, unable to avoid the inevitable. The last thing he saw on this earthly plain was a blinding flash.

The explosion was deafening. The shock wave radiated out from the Al Aqsa Mosque, violently shaking everything for blocks.

On the rooftop, the Prime Minister and Fatima had to steady themselves to keep from falling. Ali held the tripod to keep the camera from tumbling over.

"What the – ?!?" It was Munson shouting in their ears. Not intentionally. Just a normal shocked human reaction to what he had just witnessed on the in-studio monitors in New York.

Debris rocketing into the sky from the mosque grabbed their attention. They had a clear view of it from their vantage point atop Herod's Palace. Fatima, ever the professional, whirled around and stared at Ali. She jerked her head toward the mosque and dome. He knew what she wanted. Gripping the camera, he focused on the source of the explosion. He was quick enough to catch debris on its downward plunge.

They all witnessed – along with the rest of the world in real time – the building crack and implode on itself.

"Yes! Yes! Good!" Munson said, trying to control his voice. "Ali, I want you to keep that camera focused on the mosque for a minute, then change over to views of the faces of the Prime Minister and Fatima. We need their reactions, especially his."

Ali rolled his eyes in disgust, knowing Munson couldn't see him. He understood the importance of the news but sometimes he felt they were no different than ambulance-chasing lawyers. And this – the destruction of the Al Aqsa Mosque – hit him hard, being a Muslim.

"Yes, sir, I won't move from this spot!" Ali replied, his tone not revealing his true feelings. His hands shook as he tried to hold the camera steady as his heart raced. He looked over at Fatima, who stood speechless at the sight. She heard rumbling from the mosque and saw smoke billowing from all sides. She remembered she was still live on the air.

"Viewers, we don't know what just happened here, but it's apparent there's been a serious explosion at this holy site," she said, trying to keep her body's shaking to a minimum.

As she and thousands from around the world watched, the mosque began falling inward, slowly at first, with chunks of debris and dust billowing into the sky. As it picked up speed, the entire building collapsed in on itself. Fatima saw dozens of people running from the building as it fell, their clothes and bodies bloodied. The Al-Aqsa Mosque, a feature on the Jerusalem landscape for hundreds of years, was no more. It was hard to take in.

She wondered how many people had died inside the structure, never having the chance to flee. She shuddered at the thought.

A second explosion rang out. Fatima heard herself scream. She saw the Prime Minister's bodyguards rush quickly to his side, their handguns at the ready.

They all saw that the second explosion came from the Dome of the Rock, another holy site. Cracks ripped through the golden dome of the ancient structure. It was so unbelievable it almost didn't look real. Just like the mosque, it caved in on itself. In seconds all that remained of both structures was a thick cloud of smoke clinging to the area.

Fatima spoke, though to her the event was so surreal it didn't even sound like her own voice. "Mr. Prime Minister, do you think this was a TRIAD attack?"

"I have no idea," he said, his tone angry. His bodyguards urged him to leave the rooftop. "We have soldiers guarding the mosque along with private security. We, Israelis, take the safety of Muslims very seriously."

"Private security? By whom?" Fatima asked, her microphone held inches from his mouth.

The look on the PM's face told Fatima he immediately regretted mentioning it.

"I have to go," he said dryly as his security detail spirited him away to the elevator. In a moment they all were gone, the steel doors slammed tightly closed.

"Private security?" Fatima asked Ali. It was a rhetorical question, not something he could really answer.

Before Ali could respond, Munson barked in their ears. "Keep rolling, Ali! Get it all! This is important stuff, and we have the lead on it. Ali, move to the edge of the roof for a better shot."

Ali silently did what he was told. Fatima helped by moving the portable monitor.

"Fatima, we'll take it from here. You can relax," Munson ordered.

"Okay," she said, shock giving way to exhaustion. Normally, she'd protest since she was the journalist on the scene, but she was too emotionally drained now.

She heard Munson command the broadcast in her earpiece. He was almost gleeful, basking in this tragedy, using it to take center stage. To make it all about himself. It sickened her. She removed the earpiece from her ear and collapsed on the bench. Her body shook violently, and salty tears streaked down her face. Fatima heard screams from the people in the streets below, which mingled with her own internal sobs. She looked over at Ali, faithfully operating the camera, following Munson's orders. She could see he too was crying. She slowly stood and walked over to him, hoping to be of aid to her friend.

She glanced at the monitor and saw the camera lens was focused on the people at ground zero as emergency vehicles arrived. That was good. All stories are human stories no matter what. Paramedics hurried about, helping the injured. Police and military teams maintained control. They cordoned off the area and closed streets, directing people and vehicles. A helicopter roared by overhead, but Fatima couldn't look away from the people. She noticed with alarm a few black SUVs with shaded windows. Armed men stood around them, dressed in black. They weren't helping anyone, nor assisting in any way. They just stood observing, machine guns in hand. Police and soldiers walked past them, almost as if their presence was normal and expected.

Stenciled on the black vehicles in small white block letters clearly designed to not draw too much attention were four words – Glass Eye Global Security.

Fatima gently tapped Ali on his left shoulder. Keeping his camera rock steady and focused on the scene below, he glanced over to her.

She pointed at the SUVs with the stenciled letters. "Could that be the company the PM was referring to?"

"Don't worry, Fatima, I can find out who they are." He held up his free hand and spoke confidently and melodramatically. "The internet and I are one."

Fatima nodded with a slight grin. She knew she could count on Ali to do his best in everything he does.

She turned her attention to the carnage below her, and her heart pounded with emotion. *Who could be behind this horrible attack?*

CHAPTER TWO

Christopher Munson's face popped up on Fatima's computer. Though Fatima was a "people person," she loved Zoom calls. It gave her the freedom to be a globetrotter and still make office meetings. It also got her away from the small-talk and office gossip she so despised. She sometimes thought that not mingling with co-workers and other general social gatherings was why she was still single. But she always pushed those thoughts out of her mind, concluding it was her mother talking. Gone several years now, her mother still influenced her thinking. She always annoyed her mother when Fatima told her she was married to her career. She often fought with her mother while growing up, as teen daughters often do, but oh, how she missed her mother now, a lump forming in her throat.

"Where are you?" Christopher asked from her computer screen.

"At the hotel room you're paying for."

He grinned. *News World* always provided the best accommodations for their on-screen talent. And this time was no different. Fatima was in a 5-star hotel with a room as spacious as an apartment, and on a floor high enough to give a breathtaking view of Jerusalem.

"Israel has shut down travel, so it looks like we're here for a while," she told him. "It's okay, though. I'm following a lead."

That piqued his interest. "What is it?"

"I'll let you know if it turns into something."

"Oh, c'mon, Fatima." Though he half expected that response, it irritated him. Fatima liked dragging out the drama of any story she was chasing, even if it included keeping the boss in the dark for a time. Christopher found it annoying and never got used to it.

"I need a little leeway right now."

"You always do this to me." He slammed his hand down on his desk.

"I know," she smiled. "Got to keep you on your toes. Have to run. I'll be in touch soon."

"Okay," Christopher sighed. He wanted to press her on the issue but let it go for now.

Fatima knew he wouldn't push her for a reply. Afterall, she was nearly six thousand miles away and could end the call with a simple cursor tab. That was another reason she liked Zoom calls over in-person meetings. It was much easier to get out of it. And that's just what she did.

"Bye now," she said as she tabbed off. She sighed as she pushed herself back from the desk and stood. She needed to get down to Ali's humbler hotel room – on a much lower floor with an underwhelming view – and see what he'd found out so far.

"A blog post?" Fatima asked, her voice filled with skepticism and disappointment.

Ali raised his hands defensively. "Now just hold on a second, Fatima."

He whirled around in his chair to face an impressive, makeshift computer workstation spread out before him in his relatively small hotel room. He'd pushed together a little desk and table to create the necessary workspace. Every square inch of the surface was covered in keyboards, hard drives, and monitors. He was like a miracle worker with electronics and computers – things he took with him no matter where he traveled.

"Blogs often slipped past the radar. A keyword here and there are like breadcrumbs leading us to where we're trying to get." He tapped a monitor that showed a webpage filled with text. "This one references a company called Glass Eye Global Security that works with Israeli military. This has to be what we're looking for."

"Who owns this company?" She leaned in closer to read the monitor.

"That's where it gets weird," Ali said as he faced her again. "I don't know. And trying to find out is like navigating an infinite maze. The person who owns the company appears to be the stereotypical riddle, wrapped in a mystery, inside an enigma."

She rolled her eyes. "I got it, I got it. I'm familiar with the Winston Churchill quote. Give it your best shot. I'm going to the bomb site to take some photos and see what I can find out."

He furrowed his brow. "You think that's really a good idea? I mean, it just happened a few hours ago. You probably can't get too close."

"You could be right," she shrugged, "but I won't know until I try."

"Sounds dangerous."

"Danger is our business," she laughed. "Thought you'd have figured that out by now."

She turned and strolled to the door, notebook, pens and cell phone tucked in her shoulder bag.

"Be careful," Ali called after her.

"Always am. See you later," she said, shutting the door behind her.

He sighed and turned back to his workstation.

As Fatima climbed behind the wheel of their rented SUV, she knew the trip was probably a waste of time. She surmised Ali was right, that she was never going to get close to the site of the explosion. She was a good investigative reporter and had often found ways to worm her way into difficult places, but this was different. Two of the world's most holy sites had just been destroyed. Even before she and Ali left Herod's Palace they could see the place crawling with emergency medical personnel, police, Israeli military, and undoubtably Israeli Intelligence. And a new entity – Glass Eye Global Security.

Yeah, I'm not going to learn anything from this venture. But I have to try.

As she pulled the SUV out of the garage and paused at a stop sign, Fatima noticed a bearded man staring at her from the opposite side of the intersection. The look in his eyes was hard and piercing, as if he was looking straight into her soul. She shuddered and immediately rationalized it away as she drove on past him.

Probably a mentally ill homeless guy staring at nothing. No… he was dressed too nice for that. Okay, so it only appeared that he was looking at me, that's all. I doubted he could even see me through the window… what with reflections and all.

Stopping at a red light at the intersection, Fatima glanced in the sideview mirror but couldn't find him. She craned her neck all the way around, to the point of discomfort, to look back behind the car. But the man was nowhere in sight. And there was nothing in the immediate vicinity he could have stepped behind to obstruct her view. It was as though he vanished into thin air. *That's strange,* she thought.

She tried to put it out of her mind as the light turned green and she stepped on the gas pedal. But the memory of the man's piercing eyes stayed with her like the shadow image one is left with after a camera light flashes.

The scene was pretty much what Fatima thought it would be. She was kept behind a barrier three blocks from the explosion, along with hundreds of others, most there just to gawk at witnessing a tragedy that would someday be in the history books and discussed in every classroom in the world.

Fatima browsed the scene for a couple of hours, snapping what pictures she could, before heading back to the hotel to see what Ali had dug up, if anything.

About 300 kilometers north of Jerusalem, and slightly to the east sat Damascus, the capital of Syria. It was the world's oldest capital and the fourth holiest city in Islam. Located in the southwestern part of the country, many have referred to it as "the pearl of the east." And many centuries ago, it was considered one of the world's paradises. Sadly, after the Syrian Civil War in the 21st century it was ranked the least livable city in the world.

That ranking notwithstanding, Damascus was the proud location of the Umayyad Mosque, also known as the Great Mosque of Damascus. It was one of the largest and oldest mosques in the world, and – like the city itself – was one of the holiest places in Islam. The magnificent mosque easily stood out on the landscape, dwarfing the buildings around it. Breathtakingly large with pillars stretched along its front, the expansive building sported spires atop it reaching to the heavens.

Inside, the mosque's highly respected Imam named Mahdi strode with purpose down a lengthy marble corridor. Mahdi was a man in his late sixties but had glistening eyes full of life and more energy than a man half his age. Dressed in a traditional Imam's robe, he normally displayed a smile atop his full beard, and still did today, but he was very troubled.

His given name, chosen by his parents, carried a great deal of weight in Islam. This would not be a big deal had he chosen another career, but becoming an Imam added to the burden of the name.

Mahdi, also known as The Mahdi, or al-Mahdi, or The Guide is a central figure in Islamic eschatology – a messianic figure – who many believe will appear at the end of times to rid the world of evil and injustice. He is believed to be a descendant of Muhammad who will appear shortly before the prophet Isa and be a leader for Muslims going forward into the future.

Though his name was absent from the Qur'an, he was mentioned in numerous hadiths, and was important to both Shi'a and Sunni branches of Islam, which is considered rare.

For 'this' Mahdi, though, all of these beliefs and views carried a weary load that, at times, produced more than its share of anxiety. There had been many times over his decades as Imam that natural disasters or world events caused by political strife led many people to believe the end was near. Which meant Mahdi would take a major role on center stage of world events. But of course, it never happened. The End Times were never ushered in.

But this time it felt different to Mahdi. What happened in Jerusalem was a man-made disaster of unimaginable proportions. And Mahdi feared things were just going to get worse.

With what seemed like the weight of the Islamic world on his shoulders, Mahdi followed his assistant Jamal toward a private chamber.

Inside, a small group of Islamic clerics sadly viewed the remains of the Dome of The Rock and the Al Aqsa Mosque on a large flatscreen television mounted on the wall.

Mahdi and Jamal joined the men and watched the smoke furling up from the destruction of the dome and the mosque.

All eyes turned to Mahdi. He was the man in charge. They knew he would know what to do. He looked from one to the other and his troubled eyes smiled, putting them a little at ease.

"I will need to address this," he said. Then, specifically to Jamal, he added, "Arrange it and let the people know."

Jamal nodded with respect and discipline. Mahdi turned and left the room as Jamal gathered the others around him.

After the dust from the bombings in Jerusalem settled with the sunset, Israeli soldiers with bomb-sniffing dogs patrolled the neighborhoods during the night to ensure no other explosive devices lingered in the shadows, ready to be triggered. The bombed-out ancient buildings were cordoned off to keep the curious and looters away. Israeli and United States troops worked side-by-side to keep order and prevent additional chaos from erupting. But there was another presence among them, working with them. It was Glass Eye Global Security. Always there, always in the background.

The next morning, the coffee shops and bakeries were filled with larger crowds than normal, though they opened for business an hour later than usual. Workers and families comforted each other in the midst of the destruction, fearful at what had occurred, wanting to reassure themselves that life would remain the same. But never before had such holy buildings been the target of terrorists, and the people wanted answers.

At 8 a.m., two businessmen from England sat at a table near the edge of the outdoor seating area at one of the newer cafes. One drank black tea, the other sipped strong black coffee. They looked out of place, dressed in gray silk suits, white shirts, and ties, while those around them were dressed in more casual, local clothing.

"Crazy stuff happening here, huh?" the bald man asked the other, rubbing the back of his neck. "I didn't sleep much last night."

"Yes," the younger man nodded. "I can't wait until this convention is over and we're back home. Never been near a bombing before and don't ever want to be again!" He shivered despite it being a balmy day.

An old man, slumped down into his seat not too far from them, stared into his mug of hot tea. "Dajjal...Dajjal... Dajjal..." he said repeatedly to no one.

The two businessmen exchanged puzzled looks. The younger man leaned in and whispered. "What is that he's saying?" He listened, then tried to pronounce it. "Da... gel?"

"It's Arabic. Dajjal – the Antichrist in Islam. Pretty strange, huh?" He laughed nervously at the reference and his companion went quiet, a somber look lingering. Neither of them was particularly religious, but the events the day before would make most people pause and consider.

The men drank the last of their brews, put money on the table and left the café, as the old man continued his solemn chant.

CHAPTER THREE

Paul Sheppard strode quickly along King Faisal Street toward the public square in Damascus. He wore dark clothing so as not to draw attention and hid his features in a black hooded sweatshirt. With the sunrays beating down from a cloudless sky, he turned off the square, down an alley, in the direction of the war-torn section of the city. He glanced back a few times to make sure he wasn't followed. The further he walked into the destroyed neighborhood, the quieter it got. He wasn't surprised. He knew it was a dangerous part of town that people tended to avoid.

He emerged onto a demolished and abandoned street, passing the remains of cars burnt black from fire, and buildings bearing massive, jagged holes from explosions. Everything told a story that no one would hear. The street was dead silent except for the occasional caw of a crow looking for whatever morsels remained from the desolation.

A few blocks on, he reached an abandoned, bombed-out building and climbed the steps to its main entrance. Once a regal structure, now gaping holes stared empty where glass windows once glistened. Upper floors on the back side were collapsed down upon those below. Gray and white pigeons flew overhead, in and out of the decrepit structure. Concrete and wood rubbish littered the street and spaces between the various buildings, which were no longer livable nor safe to former residents. Yet some made homes deep inside the broken structures, having nowhere else to go.

Paul walked up to the heavy set of double doors at the top of the stairs and knocked. Though discolored from burns, it remained solid and closed. After a minute, two guards carrying rifles opened the doors. Paul tossed his hood back and flashed a badge, which they scanned, and allowed him inside, indicating by a nod of their heads which direction he was to go. Signs posted in both English and a foreign language marked the hallway, which was remarkably restored, the marble tiles of the floor relatively clean but for concrete dust piled in the corners. At the end of the hallway was a wooden door marked "Glass Eye Global Security." He entered a room filled with simple black desks holding computer monitors and keyboards, and walls punctuated with large black TV screens. A man dressed in a white shirt, navy blue tie, and dark slacks rose from his chair to greet him. The tie hung loosely around his collar; the badge pinned tightly to his shirt pocket. It read "David Tonklin."

"Ah, it's good to see you, Paul," Tonklin said, extending his hand. He stood a few inches taller and was a slighter build than his acquaintance. "You're a bit late, though. The CIA wait 'til the last minute to send you again?" he grinned.

Paul returned the handshake and shrugged. "Yes, as usual. Got here as soon as I could."

Tonklin laughed. "Well, I'm just glad they sent you. You'll be working with me now, at least, temporarily. As an advisor. And you arrived just in time. Come, take a look over here." Tonklin moved to the wall of screens, which showed various views from the air of a small building crammed in between other larger buildings.

"What's this?" Paul asked, pondering what he'd just heard, not sure he wanted to work for Tonklin. "Seems to be just another empty building."

"Watch the screens. It's a grade school, but intel says it's a TRIAD stronghold. Courtesy of our upgraded security clearance," Tonklin explained.

Paul looked confused. "Intel says? Really? Our intel hasn't even found out who the leader of TRIAD is. Why would we trust it on this info? And why is the U.S. military out-sourcing this anyway? Why is Glass Eye involved?"

"Well… the CIA, along with every other U.S. agency is pretty busy since the terrorist attack on Jerusalem yesterday."

"Yes, I know. Everyone on the planet is on high alert. But the U.S. military has plenty of resources – even under current conditions – to handle this. So why aren't they?"

Tonklin hesitated, then finally shrugged. *What the Hell, I guess Paul should know*, he thought.

"Plausible deniability," he admitted.

"Which means they're unsure of the intel," Paul said, concerned. It was a comment, not a question. It put Tonklin on the spot, so he ignored it. But Paul dug in. "Right?"

Tonklin raised both hands, palms up. "We've only seen adults come and go."

Paul walked closer to one of the screens to get a better look. He could see the adjacent buildings were attached, or so close as to be touching. "They could easily enter through the connecting buildings, and we wouldn't see it from the air."

Tonklin smiled and shook his head. "Getting cold feet, Paul?" He walked over to stand next to him. He looked like a tiger ready to pounce on its evening dinner of deer meat.

Paul glanced at him, annoyed. *Cold feet? Oh, please.* Paul knew Tonklin liked his kills clean. Sanitized. Seen from a safe distance with a cup of coffee in his hands. *Try being a field agent where you might have to dish out death up close and personal. Maybe you'd think twice about it then.*

"I just want to be sure," Paul said blankly. "After all, I am the 'advisor,' right?"

Tonklin brushed his hand through his hair and impatiently turned away. "Paul, that's just a figurehead position. I've been given full authority to do what I deem necessary, no matter what it involves. Truth be told, I'm the one in charge here."

The men turned to watch the screens as they saw movement. Several black SUVs approached the building and about a dozen people got out of the vehicles. They were all dressed in black robes with hoods.

Tonklin grinned ear to ear. "It's showtime."

A technician seated at the other end of the room stood to get their attention. "The drones are moving into position, sir."

Paul tried one last time. "Let me lead a team on the ground to gather more intel. Should only take an hour or so at the most." He felt an anxiety pang in his stomach.

"We have all the intel we need, Paul."

"But–"

"Drones are in position now," the technician called out.

Tonklin shouted without hesitation – "Fire!" – pointing his hands at the screens.

The muscles of Paul's face tightened as he controlled his anger, feeling helpless to stop what was happening. He watched the monitors closely, shifting his gaze from one to another. He silently prayed the target wasn't a school. He saw those on the ground near the vehicles look up in horror as the missiles struck their target; the explosion sending debris and clouds of dust flying into the air along with body parts. As the clouds dissipated, Paul saw the aftermath. The SUVs were smoldering hunks of metal. Dead, burning bodies were scattered in various positions on the ground around them. The building's framework of metal beams protruded at angles, no longer capable of holding up the structure. Fire burned from inside the building, sending billows of smoke skyward.

Just as Paul started to turn away from the scene, his gaze caught something moving. *Oh, no, not this.* A young hand reached from beneath a small pile of rubble. A bloody face appeared, and the mouth shaped a silent scream. It was a little boy. His clothes torn and bloody, he crawled out and fell with a thud onto his back in front of one of the vehicles.

Tonklin said not a word but stood with his hands on his hips in front of the array of screens. He looked pleased with himself and ignored the images that looked to be children. He stood for a long time, deep in his own thoughts.

Paul exchanged solemn looks with a technician before heading to the door.

"Where are you going, Sheppard?" Tonklin asked as he glanced back. He knew he screwed this up, but he wasn't one to shy away from a conflict. He braced himself for Paul's reaction. Instead, Paul ignored him and passed through a hidden exit onto a rusty balcony.

The metal railing jangled as he leaned over it and vomited to the street two stories below, hoping to rid his soul of the massacre he just witnessed. Paul wasn't a stranger to death, not at all. He'd seen plenty of it as a CIA field agent. But this? *I should have stopped Tonklin. What was I thinking?*

Across the street, a bearded man who appeared to be in his fifties, wearing a black tunic, stood silently. He watched Paul retch for a minute, content with the scene. In fact, he seemed to bask in Paul's anguish, as if getting sustenance from it. Satisfied, the bearded man turned and walked in the direction of the public square before he disappeared.

CHAPTER FOUR

Last night, after Fatima returned from the sites of the two explosions, she checked on Ali's progress in his search for any information about Glass Eye Global Security. Ali was in his room, deep in his search through the worldwide web – including the dark web – but had yet to turn up anything of real note. While he did that, Fatima called people in the United States, where it was still business hours. All were happy to take her call, knowing she was the woman practically at ground zero in Jerusalem and on the air to boot when the horrifying deeds took place.

Ali interrupted her calls, shouting, "I found something! Here, take a look at this." Fatima put down her phone and listened to Ali.

He'd had a breakthrough on the dark web. A name associated with the security company popped up: Richard Abramov. The pair read what was on the screen.

Abramov owned Glass Eye Global Security. And there was another revelation. He was one of the wealthiest men on the planet. Possibly even the wealthiest. But there was a catch – almost no one knew he existed.

"I've never heard of him, "Fatima said.

"Neither have I, "Ali said, shaking his head.

A quick call to Christopher Munson revealed he'd never heard of him either, which was a surprise. It was Munson's job to know everything.

"It might be possible for the richest man in the world to hide his identity," Fatima speculated. Deep pockets had a way of accomplishing a lot of things. However, in this modern era of the information superhighway, of everyone being connected to everyone else, it seemed unlikely. He hadn't been able to completely hide himself, but he did a darned good job.

Though they'd found Abramov and discovered he was the owner of Glass Eye, they found very little else. They couldn't find his lineage, his age, or even a photo, which was the most mind-blowing part of it when one considered it was the 21st century. Pictures of anyone or anything could be discovered on the internet.

Fatima quietly uttered the name "Richard Abramov" to herself, meticulously enunciating each syllable as if hoping that saying it aloud would bring clarity to his identity. Lost in thought, she paced back and forth behind Ali, who remained seated, hunched over his keyboard and monitors. "How could he keep his likeness off the internet?"

"I have no idea, but it's a pretty amazing feat," Ali said as he rotated his chair around to face her. "Oh, but there's more," he added with a wide, dramatic grin, the kind one gives when they have a winning poker hand.

"Well, don't keep me in suspense."

"Looking into this guy was like pulling a loose thread on a shirt and unraveling the whole thing."

Ali laughed at his own "clever" comment, which just drew Fatima's ire. She didn't have to say anything, her impatient glare was all Ali needed to continue.

"He seems to own everything: software companies, media companies, top companies in every industry you can imagine. Everything. He even owns companies that supply computer control systems for military applications to almost every country." Ali continued to scroll down the screen.

Fatima plopped down in the cushioned chair and sighed in exasperation.

"How is that possible, Ali? If that was the case, everyone on the planet should have heard of him." She shook her head. "This sounds like a bad conspiracy theory. And you know how we news people hate those."

She stood and poured herself a cup of coffee from a pot Ali had on a side table. She took a sip and got lost in thought.

"What is it?" Ali asked.

"You know… the Dome of the Rock is a Muslim holy site."

"Well, duh," he laughed.

She ignored the comment and went on. "Some religions… well, Christians mostly… believe its destruction will signal the start of the End Times."

Ali was amused and a little surprised. "Is that what you believe?"

"Of course not. I'm not a Christian."

"Are you a Muslim, like me?"

She almost responded with a harsh snap but caught herself. She gave a contemplative sigh and returned her gaze to the dark streets below.

By her upbringing, Fatima was a Muslim, but her beliefs and prayers faltered after her parents divorced when she was eight years old. It was then her mother stopped taking Fatima to the mosque. Then her faith was severely tested when she went to Saudi Arabia for college and stayed with her uncle, a strict mullah who, in Fatima's view, taught a distorted and dangerous view of Islam. And then when her mother died, Fatima stopped believing in Allah entirely.

She turned sad eyes to Ali. He immediately felt guilty for asking the question.

"You know the answer to that, Ali," she said so low it was barely audible. "I was raised one, but I'm not one anymore. And I certainly don't believe in the End Times."

She took another sip of coffee and sat back down in the comfortable chair. "Besides, the End Times scenario doesn't make any sense."

"How so?"

"Think about it. Wouldn't the Devil – Iblis – read the holy books and know how it's going to end?"

Ali smiled at her, impressed partially by her logic, but more so that she knew, or maybe remembered, Iblis – the

Islamic name for what the Christians would call the Devil, or Satan.

"That's a good point, Fatima. If you don't mind me asking – what do you believe?"

"I believe in nothing," she said without hesitation.

Ali's cheerful demeanor vanished, replaced by a serious and somber mood.

"I believe in the End Times. I believe that Isa will return to battle the Dajjal."

Fatima nodded solemnly; her expression tinged with indifference as she shrugged.

"C'mon, Fatima," Ali chuckled. "You've got to believe in something."

Fatima stood and ran her fingers through her hair. "I believe in myself. Now, where can we find this Richard Abramov? Assuming he really exists."

"Oh, he exists all right. He has mansions and such everywhere."

Ali swiveled his chair to face his electronic setup. With a few keystrokes his monitors filled with multiple angles of a stunning, majestic palace. Fatima was astonished at the sight of the building and its surrounding structures and rolling hills. It looked more like a university campus, except very ancient. Far older than any campus on the planet.

Ali tapped his index finger on the largest monitor, which displayed the front of the palace, its massive, circular driveway, and an impressive fountain.

"This is his place right here in Israel, just outside Jerusalem. He's easy to find. He just keeps a very low profile. Wants no fanfare. In fact, he's hosting a social event this coming weekend. A private party. Right here at his palace." He tapped the screen again to punctuate his last comment.

Fatima pushed herself out of the chair and walked over to the hotel window. She glanced down at the street and noticed there was not much traffic. *It's not just the lateness of the hour,* she thought. *People are hunkered down in their homes due to the destruction of the Dome of The Rock and Al Aqsa Mosque. Driven indoors by fear.*

"I've seen that look before, Fatima. What's on your mind?"

"A guy that powerful might use the world like a chess board. And he had the private security contract for one of the world's most sensitive spots."

"An inside job?" Ali asked, his brow furrowed.

"Just a thought," Fatima said as she quickly turned and faced him. "I have to get into this private party somehow. But I can't do it as a journalist. He's avoided attention for a reason."

Ali loved a challenge. In fact, some would say he lived for it. "I'm on it," he said with a grin smeared across his face as he leaped into action, rapidly tapping away at his keyboard.

"It's late. You should get some sleep and start in the morning."

"Nope. I don't need sleep." He continued typing.

"Okay," Fatima said with a laugh. "But I do, so I'm going up to my room and get some shut-eye."

As she left the room, she knew Ali would only work a couple more hours before he grabbed some sleep. He was driven but he wasn't stupid. And she needed him to be sharp for what might lie ahead for both as they chased down the truth of this Richard Abramov, and whether or not he was involved in the horrible terrorist attack that happened less than twelve hours ago.

Fatima woke with a start. The sun shone brightly in her hotel room from where it peeked over the horizon. She must have been too tired to draw the blinds when she returned to the room, she reasoned. All she remembered was quickly changing into her pajamas before falling into bed. Still feeling exhausted, she yanked the blinds closed then returned to the bed, but it was already too late. Her sleep was disturbed, and it didn't look like it was willing to return.

She fired up her tablet to see the latest from *News World's* website as she always did before jumping in the shower. What she saw shocked her. It was a news story less than an hour old. She could read the article, but why when there was a link to Christopher Munson at his anchor desk delivering the news?

She clicked on the link and Christopher popped into motion.

"Missiles fired minutes ago from several drones today in Damascus struck a grade school," he said as he stared straight into the camera lens. "The numbers of the dead and injured are unknown at this time. Also, unknown is whether or not the school doubled as a TRIAD cell. This is a developing story. We will give updates on the situation as we learn more."

The clip ended. Fatima was more interested in what was *not* said. *No mention of who fired the missiles. Was it the U.S.? The Syrian military? Was it somehow related to what happened in Jerusalem? If the school was housing a TRIAD cell, was this attack on it in retaliation for the Al Aqsa Mosque and Dome of the Rock? A little tit-for-tat so to speak? And if so, that means someone – be it a government agency or an individual – knows that TRIAD was behind the destruction of the Holy sites, even if it hasn't been officially declared.*

What troubled her the most was that her mind kept returning to Glass Eye Global Security. *Were they involved somehow?* But that made no sense. She was just letting her mind run wild now. She only learned about the company yesterday. Thinking they're behind any terrorist attack, much less every terrorist attack, made her sound like exactly the kind of person she couldn't stand – a conspiracy theorist.

Still, the company was owned by Richard Abramov, a man who was an enigma that accomplished what should be impossible in the 21st Century – remaining hidden beyond the ever-present and always prying eyes of the worldwide web.

The thought was troubling and filled her with fear as to what kind of man could be so powerful and influential.

CHAPTER FIVE

U.S. soldiers were on point, patrolling the grounds around the burned-out school building. Emergency medical workers from Syria and U.S. medics stationed there tended to the injured adults and children. Sirens blared while flashing emergency lights surrounded the scene, as police officials kept the crowds back. It was controlled chaos. Dozens of adults cried in anguish, while others stood silent with looks of shock on their faces. Clothing on some were torn, covered in soot from the explosion, faces dirtied by the blast. One by one, small and large stretchers holding bodies covered with dark, heavy blankets were carried away by medical teams and put into ambulances. Smoke billowed slowly from the caved-in roof of the school as firefighters worked inside to quench the last of the flames.

Though Paul knew he needed to be on the job, this was one he never liked. He had to control his pain, outrage, and frustration; there would be alone time for dealing with it later. He walked closer to the yellow-taped perimeter and showed his CIA badge to the woman standing guard, a U.S. Army cap pulled low over her forehead, her fatigues wet with sweat. She looked directly into Paul's eyes, showing no emotion. He knew inside she was likely as angry as he was. The guard nodded in silence and raised the tape to let him enter the scene.

"I'm so sorry. This was so wrong," Paul said quietly to himself. He glanced at a woman and man nearby, who held a crying, injured girl. The mother cried too, while the father comforted the child. Paul guessed her to be about seven years old. She had blood on her face and cuts on her arms. She tightly clutched a doll whose face and torn dress were covered in ash and soot. There was a table placed about six feet away, its top covered with bottles of water and small towels. He picked up three bottles and a towel before walking over to the family.

"Here, let me help," he said, handing each of them a bottle of water. He gave the towel to the father, who smiled kindly and nodded. The mother quickly drank the water, while the little girl only took a small sip from the bottle her father offered. None said a word to Paul and pulled back away from him.

"Please. I'm here to help however I can. Do either of you speak English?" he asked the parents. He could have spoken Arabic to them, but he had learned foreigners who spoke the local's language oftentimes raised suspicions. They were cagey enough as it was.

"Yes, somewhat," the father said with a heavy accent. "Why are you here? Are you one of those responsible for this?" He pointed behind him to the damaged school, then kissed his daughter on her forehead. Tear tracks were the only clean lines on his face, he too had been caught in the aftermath of the explosion.

Paul exhaled deeply. He had no words to express what was in his heavy heart. *Responsible?* Not directly. But he hadn't stopped Tonklin from ordering the strike. Paul looked into the father's eyes with an unspoken expression of sorrow.

"I'm sorry," he said. "I wouldn't blame you if you hated us, the USA, and all it represents."

The father sat taller as he handed the girl over to her mother. He turned back to Paul.

"No, we don't hate you Americans, Westerners. Hatred becomes engraved upon one's heart," he explained. "Yes, this is painful. Yes, we shed tears. Yes, we are tempted with desires to retaliate. However, it's best to write the bad things such as this event of today in the sand. That way, they can be easily erased from memory. Put your mind at ease. All this is meant to happen. It is a sign of the End Times – and the imminent return of Isa." There was a glow in his eyes despite his anguish about his daughter's injuries. "Isa. Who you would refer to as Jesus."

"You believe in Jesus?" Paul's voice cracked in surprise at hearing the father's words.

"Yes," the man said proudly. Now his eyes seemed to glow a bit brighter.

Paul couldn't believe what he was hearing. He didn't expect to hear this from a Muslim. "I'm not a religious man – but your reference to Jesus, or rather, Isa; are you Christians?"

"No, we are Muslims," the man said, shaking his head. "Isa is a most significant figure in our religion too. As is his mother, Maryam, who Christians call Mary. And Yahya, who is referred to as John the Baptist in Christianity. But he didn't baptize anyone as there is no baptism in Islam."

"This is something I've never heard before," Paul said as he furrowed his brow, processing the information.

The man nodded. "Isa is our Messiah. We believe that he will return to battle the Dajjal during the End Times. Dajjal is our word for what Christians call the 'Antichrist.'"

"This is astounding to me," Paul said, brushing his hair back off his forehead.

Even under this dire situation, the man mustered a warm smile. "Muslims revere and honor Isa as the Christians do. We believe he will return again to Earth, just like the Christians profess." He and his wife exchanged smiles, both hugging their daughter tighter.

Paul's eyes widened with wonder and curiosity. He looked at the mother, who was nodding in agreement with her husband. Her tears had stopped flowing. Long strands of dark hair had escaped from her head covering and her brightly colored tunic was soiled with some of her daughter's blood. The girl's eyes were closed as she lay in comfort on her mother's lap.

The man stood and put his hand on Paul's shoulder.

Paul relaxed, not sure what to say. "I had no idea there are those similarities between Christianity and Islam. Muslims revere Jesus? That's wonderful. Why don't Christians know this?"

"Politics has created too much division between the faiths. Not just with Islam and Christianity, but with Judaism too.

Isa is our Messiah. And although the Jews don't believe he is theirs, they too are waiting for a Messiah. Isa is the missing connection between all three Abrahamic faiths." The chaos around them seemed to grow quieter, the blaring sirens coming to a halt.

Paul was flabbergasted. "We should all be talking about the similarities instead of the differences. It could possibly alleviate so much suffering."

"Yes, that is correct." He squatted down next to his wife. "But good news doesn't sell," he said solemnly. He tenderly stroked his daughter's forehead.

Paul knew the man was right. Turn on the television or pick up a newspaper and it is all bad news. Though Paul didn't believe in Isa, or Jesus as Christians referred to him, and didn't have faith in anything spiritual, he believed that if those who did hold such beliefs could come together and find unity in their similarities, it might lead to a more peaceful world.

The man looked sad. "So much turmoil in the world." Then, with hope in his voice he said, "Most people don't know that about the Islamic faith. Isn't it time we tell them, somehow?"

Paul nodded. But he was skeptical. *How do you make a stubborn and violent world listen?*

Nearby, people lined the emergency tape strung around the area, moaning in despair as they gawked at yet another disaster caused either by a terrorist bombing or the military. At this point they didn't know who was responsible, and most were aware they may never get the answer as the Syrian government tended to be very tightlipped about such things.

Yet there was one among them who absolutely knew what was going on. It was the bearded man, ever-present. He inhaled deeply as if getting sustenance from the anguish and hopelessness that clung to the area. It was satisfying. He glanced with curiosity over at Paul Sheppard. *What a fool*, he thought. A man who tried to help but knew nothing about how the universe really worked.

He breathed in the smell of the carnage again. Once the bearded man's soul was filled with the feast this scene of gloom provided, he turned and slipped through the crowd. As soon as he was out of sight he disappeared. As if he were never there.

CHAPTER SIX

Under a black, star-filled night sky loomed the Umayyad Mosque in Damascus. It was Saturday night and crowds filled the front steps and courtyard. Imam Mahdi planned to recite words from the Qur'an to the Muslims gathered inside for prayers. After the bombings in Jerusalem, many gathered for fellowship and to comfort each other. It was standing room only for those fortunate enough to get into the building. The people were of all ages, and all were anxious.

"Thank you all for coming to the khutbah this evening," Mahdi said into the microphone mounted on the podium, his voice filling the mosque while echoing for blocks from the large amplifiers mounted outside in front of the mosque.

He turned his attention to his Qur'an and took a breath before continuing. "I read from Surah Al Baqarah. 'And when it is said to them, "Do not make trouble on Earth," they say, "We are only reformers." In fact, they are the troublemakers, but they are not aware. And when it is said to them, "Believe as the people have believed," they say, "Shall we believe as the fools have believed?" In fact, it is they who are the fools, but they do not know.

'And when they come across those who believe, they say, "We believe;" but when they are alone with their devils, they say, "We are with you; we were only ridiculing."

'It is God who ridicules them and leaves them bewildered in their transgression. Those are they who have betrayed error for guidance; but their trade does not profit them, and they are not guided. Their likeness is that of a person who kindled a fire, when it illuminated all around him, God took away their light and left them in darkness, unable to see. Deaf, dumb, blind. They will not return.'"

The worshipers knelt; their heads bowed to the ground. Upon hearing the Imam's voice continue, they raised up again and listened.

"We do not know who committed the bombings in Jerusalem. We can suspect it was TRIAD, those who have turned their backs on the true tenets of Islam. To build up their forces, they will likely gather the unemployed and thugs of the city in the name of Islam and Shariah. Then they will continue to spread butchery and terrorism in the world. But we gathered here, we are not part of that." The Imam bowed low as did the others.

After a few moments, he continued. "Never forget that this is the battle of the Lord of the universe and not ours. The Lord considers the death of one man equivalent to the death of humanity. This is why we must avoid feud and warfare under all circumstances. However, Islam allows one to attack back the enemy like the Lion of God if the enemy leaves you with no choice."

The people in the crowd nodded, bowed on the floor to God for a final time, then rose to leave the mosque after they greeted the Imam one by one.

The Imam spoke loudly as they quietly walked out of the room. "Never forget! We have set out to diminish the darkness of ignorance through the light of knowledge. We have set out to defeat the mischief makers through our invitation of peace. We want to surround them in the ground of knowledge and intellect, peace, safety, and brotherhood. But they want to drag us into the ground of bomb blasts and killings. All praise be to Him who grants an individual the strength to guide and another to receive guidance."

As the people rose in praise, commotion from outside grabbed everyone's attention. Imam Mahdi quickly hurried through the crowd toward the front doors. *Oh no, are we under attack now as well?*

Outside, the crowd stared in awe into the night sky, a cool but rising breeze ruffled the leaves of the surrounding trees. Phone cameras came up to record whatever it was that had captured their attention.

Mahdi joined the crowd and squinted skyward. He gasped. And for one of the very few times in the Imam's life, he was speechless.

CHAPTER SEVEN

In the two days since the bombings, nothing more had been learned about who was responsible or whether any other historical sites might be in danger. Israel had stepped up its patrols and soldiers walked the streets around the clock for citizens' protection. Fatima and Ali talked with Jerusalem residents when they were allowed, gathering opinions and conducting on-camera interviews, the topic uppermost in the world's mind. Back in New York, Munson was pleased that two of his best staff people were on the ground in Jerusalem; ratings for the news show climbed to a new high in those few days.

And Ali wasn't boasting when he said "I'm on it" to Fatima a few days ago. He met up with two men with whom he went to college. One was a brilliant software engineer named Tim who made far more money as a consultant, rather than being tied down to a stuffy corporate office. He was a slim, unimposing guy, a wallflower at any party, but he could do great things – or great damage if he wanted – with his computer skills. The other fellow was a larger, intimidating guy, a Jewish man named Noah, who was vague on his career path following college. Rumor had it he either currently worked for the Mossad or did at one time. Ali never pressed him on it and the guy never volunteered an answer. Didn't matter, though. Ali and Noah were good friends in college, and he came when Ali requested his presence. As did Tim. Ali asked them for help, and they obliged.

Noah confirmed what Ali had already discovered – that Abramov lived right here in Jerusalem, in a palace no less, and was this week due to have an international party there. With Abramov's pull, he could get the Israeli government to look the other way as guests flew in on private jets, violating the no-fly restrictions set after the terrorist attack.

Fatima just couldn't get over the fact that Abramov could pull off such a feat, even with his wealth and power. Or that he would even want to do something like that.

"Wow!" Fatima said to Ali, who sat across from her at a nearby cafe. "Having a big party doesn't sound like a guy who's trying to keep a low profile."

"Except it's not in the news."

She was perplexed. "How could he pull that off? I've learned in the news business that the more people you have involved in anything, the less likely it can be kept a secret. Especially something like a big party with wealthy people. This is the kind of thing the tabloids would go crazy over."

"True. But somehow, he's managed to get a news blackout on it. If I hadn't glimpsed it on the dark web, we still wouldn't know about it. In fact, I can't even find it now."

"What do you mean?"

"Someone scrubbed it off the web. We just got lucky I guess."

"Wow," she said again, this time so low it was almost inaudible. Although she was impressed that Richard Abramov managed to run this far beneath the radar, she was even more impressed that Ali was able to discover it before it disappeared.

On Saturday morning, about ten hours before Mahdi would look into the night sky and witness something that would change his life forever, Ali summoned Fatima to his hotel room.

She was shocked at what he handed her upon her arrival.

"Really? Fake ID?" she said incredulously, staring at her own photo with the name SHEILA BOWMAN beneath it. "How did you do this?"

"Better not to know," he said with a nod and wink. It was Noah's doing, but the less said the better. "I'm sure it will be good enough to get you into the party. In fact, you are already on the guest list under the name Sheila Bowman, Director of the Old Jerusalem Preservation Society. Which means you are not going as a reporter, so you can't ask him questions."

She shrugged, a little disappointed. "Okay, well at least I'll see what he looks like and hopefully learn something about him just by being there."

"You will be wearing a hidden microphone, so you can talk to me and be safe if anything goes wrong."

"What could go wrong?" Fatima wasn't so sure about playing spy anymore.

"Nothing. Everything. I don't know, I'm just a videographer for a news agency. You're going to be in a room full of elites and powerful people. But I'll be nearby in a van with my two college buddies." Ali gave her a reserved, forced smile, then turned away and buried his face in his computer equipment, which looked more like a small television station control room.

His actions didn't fool Fatima for a second. "What's wrong?" she asked.

He slowly swiveled back around to face her. "Fatima, you need to be sure about this trip," he said, his voice low. "If this guy is as powerful as he seems to be, you can't get caught pretending to be someone else. If he's not well known internationally with all the business that he does, there must be a reason for it. I'd hate to see you get hurt…or killed."

Fatima breathed deeply and walked over to Ali. Putting her hand on his shoulder, she said, "I'd be lying if I said I wasn't nervous about this, but think about it, this is the chance of a lifetime. An opportunity for us truly to be investigative journalists in deep cover. International intrigue. Secrets. Vastly wealthy people."

She grew silent for a moment, lost in thought. "Ali, I became a reporter to learn about other people's lives and to visit other countries, other cultures. I have to do this. We've just witnessed a Muslim holy mosque and the Dome of the Rock destroyed this week. That's huge! They had stood for thousands of years! You know… I got to know quite a few Christians while going to high school in the U.S. As I mentioned before, many of them believe its destruction will signal the beginning of the End Times." She let that information sink in before continuing. "What does the End Times really mean?"

"Not sure what to think about the End Times, but I believe we all have a purpose in life, whether Jewish, Christian, Muslim, or any other religion." he said. "I don't know what our purpose is, but I'm happy that you and I are discovering what's meant for both of us here at this time."

She looked him directly in the eyes. "Well, I don't know what greater purpose in life we may or may not have, but my purpose tonight is to see if I can find out if Glass Eye Global Security, and hence Abramov, is behind the destruction of the Al Aqsa Mosque and the Dome of the Rock. If it's a dead-end, well, nothing ventured, nothing gained. Are you in?"

He got up, hugged Fatima and said, "Absolutely. And I'll be sure you're safely wired for the party. We're a team, remember? 'Sheila Bowman…Director of the Old Jerusalem Preservation Society.' That has a nice ring to it."

Fatima playfully punched him on the arm. "Got to go shopping now for an elegant dress. I'll see you around dinner time." She waved to him as she closed the hotel room door behind her.

Once Ali heard the door click shut, his smile faded, and he plopped down on the couch. He didn't want to worry Fatima with what he was really thinking. *Could this truly be the beginning of the End Times? With all the continuing terrorist attacks, and now this – the destruction of the Al Aqsa Mosque and Dome of the Rock? And if it is indeed the End Times, it means it's time for the Dajjal – the Antichrist – to fully make his presence known.*

His mind wandered to the words of the Prophet regarding the Kharijites, and he spoke them aloud to himself. "Every time a generation of them appears it will be cut down – this will occur over twenty times – until the Antichrist appears in their last remnant."

This latest group of Kharijites – TRIAD – is the most vicious to date. Will their very presence bring about the Dajjal?

He paled at the thought.

✳   ✳   ✳

Ali had arranged for a limousine to pick up Fatima at the hotel and drive her to the party. He had decided it would be best to maneuver a communications van within range of Abramov's mansion in order to stay in touch with her by microphone. Ali felt comfortable having Tim and Noah with him in the van. He felt they made a good team.

Dressed in a black sequined, knee-length gown that showed off her trim figure, Fatima looked appropriate and stunning in her high heels, dark hair pinned on top of her head, and a clutch bag in her hand. The limo's window between her and the driver was closed tightly when Ali's voice called to her.

"Can you hear me, Fatima?" Ali asked.

"Yes, loud and clear," she whispered, relaxing into the soft leather seat as she gazed out the limo's window.

"Move your purse a bit – let me check the camera," he told her.

Fatima obliged by pointing the clutch to give him an outside view.

"Good. It's working fine. You'll make it through Abramov's security with no problem. The camera is sewn into the purse and the few metal parts will blend in with its zipper. Don't give it a thought, carry it like you normally would."

"Sounds good. Thank you, Ali, for taking such good care of me in this," Fatima said. She was grateful for his friendship.

"Teamwork. That's what we do. Okay, it won't be long before the limo has you at the mansion. Just relax and enjoy the party. Don't overstep things but use your reporter's instincts. You got this, girl," Ali said.

Fatima took a deep breath to steady her nerves. As they approached the mansion, Fatima was overwhelmed by its beauty. She checked her lipstick in the small mirror in her clutch, looked at her hair one last time, and let herself feel the excitement of what was to come. *This is going to be some event. Mr. Abramov, who are you? What is your goal here? Are you a player in what happened in Jerusalem?*

The limo driver pulled to a slow stop at the foot of the mansion's steps where a man dressed in a black suit and white gloves carefully opened the car door for Fatima. She handed him her identification card, and he checked the guest list on his tablet, confirming her name and invitation. *Ali's friends were good.*

"Welcome, Miss Bowman. We are happy to have you," the attendant said as he bowed. "Please follow the other gentleman to the top of the stairs where you will be directed to the ballroom."

Fatima tipped her head in thanks and held firmly onto the clutch as she mounted the set of stairs. As she got closer to the entry door, she heard lively music from inside. A male singer, reminiscent of Frank Sinatra, was singing a familiar tune as trumpets and violins accompanied him. She heard laughter and loud voices conversing from an outside patio located to the far left. Lights were strung from trees at the patio, and the lighting from inside the home through its beveled-glass door made it a festive sight. A cool breeze blew tree branches along the staircase, which were trimmed to create an archway over the steps at the home's entry.

"All's well," Ali whispered from the van. "Just take your time, take it slow."

Fatima smiled as she entered the room, feeling good that Ali and his team had her back. A woman wearing a red-and-black dress who stood to the side of the entry door handed her a red rose, which she touched to her nose to inhale its aroma. She was emboldened as she picked up a small glass of red wine from a waiter's passing tray. She had no intention of drinking it; the wine was merely a prop to help support and maintain her alias as she moved through Abramov's party. In her days as a devout Muslim, she abstained from alcohol and continued the practice even after drifting away from her faith, more out of habit than belief. Even when faith no longer anchored her, she held steadfast to the rule of avoiding alcohol, and even pork, though the days of losing her faith felt like a distant memory.

Across the room a small orchestra was positioned on a stage built into the room's décor. Red velvet curtains flanked either side of the platform, and large white speakers hung from the ceiling, along with a projection screen built into the wall off to the side for a better, close-up view of the performers from across the room. The man singing had a wonderful baritone voice, and Fatima stood alone for a minute, taking in the sounds and ambiance of the room. She had never quite been in a place like this before.

Hundreds of people smiled, danced and ate hors d'oeuvres which were served by men dressed in black tuxedoes wearing deep blue cummerbunds and shiny black shoes.

Fatima took the time to look at the other guests and was overwhelmed with who she saw – world leaders, even a few businesspeople whom she had interviewed in years past. Powerful people, wealthy heads of state. All laughing, smiling, here at the invitation of Abramov. *Who is this man? Why the party?* All the faith-based conversations she'd had with Ali came to mind. *Was Abramov a Jew, Christian, or Muslim? Or… other?*

She slowly stepped from group to group, staying in the background, being sure to blend in with the other guests. After enjoying two tasty hors d'oeuvres, alone near a server, she felt comfortable enough to ask him to point out Abramov.

"Why, miss, you're standing not far from him," the waiter said. "He's the one talking to the group of sheiks right over there," gesturing to Abramov's back.

In her earpiece, Ali cautioned her. "What do you plan to say to him, Fatima? Be careful!" He could see Abramov through the clutch's camera, a tall man with dark hair, whose presence filled the video screen larger and larger as Fatima got closer to him. With every step forward, snow started to splay over the video and static slowly filled the audio track. Ali double-checked the wire connections in the van. "Fatima, the picture and sound...we're cutting out...something's interfering..."

The clarity of Ali's voice turned to static in her ear. She reached up and pulled the receiver from her ear, tucking it into her clutch, no longer able to hear Ali's voice.

Fatima continued her trek toward Abramov, his back still turned to her. He seemed so far away in this massive room. This ballroom. In fact, it didn't seem like she was getting closer. She picked up her pace.

In an instant, something strange happened. Sounds became muted and time seemed to slow down. She could still hear people talking and laughing, but it just wasn't very loud. Everyone was moving in slow-motion. A woman dancing to the band spun around and her dress whipped about her, taking forever to complete a turn, like the little ballerina on a music box.

Then Fatima reached him. Richard Abramov. Finally.

He turned toward her, slowly and methodically, but not because he was affected by the slowed time that held everyone else, but because he chose to. He looked her directly in the eyes and she was forced to look away, cowering in his dominant and commanding presence. He was young, and he was old. He was well-groomed with a close-cropped beard. He was wise and charismatic. But there was a hint of something else. Something he worked hard to keep hidden. Only to reveal it when the time was right. And on his terms.

Was he evil personified? She shook her head, trying to clear the cluttered thoughts from it as one would try to clear an alcohol haze. Yet, she hadn't had any alcohol. Not tonight, not ever. *What's happening to me?*

She fought her fear and focused on him as best she could. *He looks familiar. Where have I seen him before?*

Then she remembered she had seen him on the street just outside her hotel in Jerusalem. She was pulling her rental car out of the garage to drive to ground zero of the bombing.

Richard Abramov was the bearded man! This man – the bearded man – looked right at her. Right through her. It was unnerving. But he looked different then – somewhat like a street person, dirty and unkempt, someone most people would want to ignore. Here, he was spotlessly clean and well-groomed, the center of attention, someone who no one could look away from.

And that's exactly what he desired – complete control over the situation. He wished to be ignored when it served his purpose, such as when he traversed the bustling streets among the masses, disguised as the bearded man. Conversely, he wanted to command attention when it suited him best, as he did now in the grand ballroom of his palace.

Looking at him now, she could sense things about him. His presence was in the world more than 2,000 years ago, carrying knowledge of Isa's time – because he was there and witnessed it all. His sharply pressed tuxedo fit the contemporary world, but his insatiable desire for power and control clashed with any goodness his image might portray. He always lived in the present moment, whenever and wherever that moment was… because he can.

"I've been waiting for you, Fatima," Abramov said with a sly smile. His words weren't evil or threatening. They were inviting. Quite inviting. Which made them far more frightening. And dangerous.

The wine glass slipped from Fatima's hand and crashed into splinters on the marble floor. She felt drugged and no longer heard sounds from other guests or music from the orchestra. They weren't just muted, they were gone. The people continued moving in slow motion as if in another dimension, but in total silence. All of them oblivious to Fatima, and her shattered wine glass on the floor. Fatima saw the singer's mouth moving, but she heard no song. She felt dizzy.

"You can be assured, my dear lady, that I am neither a Jew, Christian, nor a Muslim. Or other," he chuckled as he said that last part. "I answer only to myself. I have read the holy books of the three Abrahamic faiths – in fact, in the original versions, not later translations." He paused to see what effect he was having on her. "And yes, the Al-Aqsa Mosque destruction as well as the Dome of the Rock was an inside job. My people – put there to protect the sites – destroyed them. But you can't prove it. Nobody can. My tracks cannot be traced, and everyone will think you're crazy. As everyone who goes against me is thought of as crazy."

Though Fatima tried to speak, her mouth would not respond to her mental efforts. His spell infused her spirit. She tried to turn away, but unlike before, when she had trouble looking at him, she now couldn't look away. He held her attention as if he had her under a hypnotic spell. She could only focus on him, hearing Abramov's voice and nothing else.

"I did it to bring about chaos and fear," he laughed. "Something I excel in. I'm the ultimate terrorist. All others are just amateurs next to me. I've had many names throughout history. I wear names like people wear clothes, and I change them as often as needed. But there is one name that has stuck with me from the beginning of time. It's not a name I gave myself; it was given to me. My true name. Al-Masih ad-Dajjal or simply Dajjal, which I prefer. It means the false messiah, the liar, the deceiver, the deceiving messiah. But who cares about such definitions? I certainly don't. I am who I am and I'm proud of it."

He let that sink in for a moment for effect.

"But enough about me. Let's talk about you," he continued, stepping closer to Fatima, looking down into her wide-open eyes. "And how you've tried to put out of your mind the brutal treatment you suffered at the hands of a relative. A man who robbed you of your faith. But I – Richard Abramov – can make you whole again, dear Fatima." He waved his arm indicating those gathered at the party. "Just as I've done with all of them. Join us, won't you? Become one of my people. You can't imagine what awaits you here." He smiled a fatherly smile which warmed her heart.

Fatima's mind flashed back to younger days, scenes spilling over, her uncle forcing his radical views upon her, and her efforts to assert herself and her individuality. And the condemning judgement of her by him and those like him. She fought off the memories, closed her eyes, trying to stay steady on her high heels. She looked Abramov in the eyes and felt safe and secure. Her past pains diminishing, fading from her mind.

Yes… he's right… maybe I can just stay here… become one of these people… they are so happy… it's so peaceful here… I would want for nothing … whiling away my days drinking and dancing… not a care or need in the world…

The thought of it gave her a sense of peace she hadn't felt in…well, possibly never.

Yet there was something at the edges of the thought she couldn't quite focus on. It was like a shadow in one's peripheral vision. When one turns to look at it, it slips away from view. It's not really gone though. It's always there. One can just never quite focus on it. She could sense it was a hateful thing. A cancer of the soul just waiting to consume her. And she'd happily let it, smiling the whole way.

No! This is wrong! Fatima came to her senses through sheer strong will. *This is evil. I need to get out of here while I still can.* Fatima squeezed her eyes shut so hard they hurt. It took a gargantuan effort to push Abramov's enticing offer from her mind. But she did it. When she opened her eyes, the music was loud and rowdy, with laughter from the crowd overpowering all other sounds.

A server appeared at her feet, carrying a small hand-broom and dustpan. He sunk to the floor to sweep up the shards of glass. Abramov had his back to Fatima, as if he had never turned around, still engaged in conversation with the sheiks.

"Would you like another drink?" the young man asked her, the traces of broken glass now taken care of. "I'd be happy to get you another."

"No, no, thank you. I'll be going now," she said as if in a daze, and then hurried toward the front door.

Richard Abramov glanced over his shoulder at her with a smirk.

"So, Richard, do you have any travel plans?" a sheik asked, drawing Abramov's attention back to the group. Though heavily accented, the sheik spoke in English for Richard's benefit. The man didn't realize it was unnecessary. Richard could speak and understand all the languages on the planet. Past, present, and future, it didn't matter. He understood every language and could speak any without a trace of an accent.

Before he could answer the sheik, his attention was drawn to the television playing over a nearby bar. On it was a young, perky female announcer from what was obviously a tabloid show. Behind her was a shaky videoclip of a silhouetted man, arms spread, descending from a star-filled night sky. Though the sound of the television was intentionally set very low, Richard could hear it clearly over all other sounds in the room.

"Video footage from a crowd gathered in Damascus has gone viral! This one in particular has already had ten million hits. It shows a man descending from the sky."

She disappeared as the clip filled the screen. Richard watched without expression as the man got larger and larger and his features appeared. The man wore a contemporary tunic, tinged with a subtle yellow hue, paired with jeans. His hairstyle was trendy, and his beard meticulously groomed.

His face radiated with a warm smile, accompanied by eyes teeming with love. The image froze, capturing the full essence of his expression as his face filled the screen. Then it shrank into a window alongside the perky announcer.

She spoke with a big, almost embarrassed grin. "There are some who are saying this is Jesus... *the* Jesus Christ... returning to Earth."

Richard's eyes subtly widen with surprise. *I thought I'd stopped this two millennia ago. Oh well. Nothing I can't deal with. The world belongs to me now.*

"Earth to Richard," the sheik said humorously, pulling Abramov's attention away from the television. It was just as well. He'd seen enough. He sighed, resolved to a course of action.

"If you'll excuse me, something pressing has come up. Something very pressing."

And with that, Richard crisply turned and strode away, leaving the perplexed sheik staring after him.

Outside at the bottom of the staircase, while Richard's attention was initially drawn to the perky young announcer on the television, Ali and the others sat parked in the van, party attendants trying to get them to pull away from the front of the mansion.

"Ali, wait!" Fatima shouted. Barefoot, she carried her high heels and clutch bag as she ran down the stairs. Guests standing beneath the trees moved out of her way as she pushed past them. Ali slid open the van's side door and she hopped into the back seat. "Go, go! Leave this place!" The van lurched forward and sped off into the night.

"Good night, guys. Thank you for your help." Fatima shook hands at the elevator with the two men who had assisted Ali in the van. Fatima and Ali rode in silence up to their rooms. Ali unlocked the door to hers and followed her inside.

"That's one wild story, Fatima," he said. "Abramov sounds insane. I don't know why we lost the audio and video signal, but the camera in your purse should have captured it all." He placed his laptop on the desk and powered it up.

Fatima handed her purse to him. She wasn't sure she wanted to witness the conversation again but was curious.

"It should all be here on the internal chip," he said, plugging it into the laptop. They watched the monitor and listened to the audio as she ascended the steps to the mansion and entered. She mingled a little, then took a glass of wine from a server's tray. All the footage was a little bouncy as she walked about, but they could still easily make out everything that she experienced.

From the monitor they heard Fatima ask the server about Richard Abramov. The server told her where he was and pointed. Then Fatima began her trek toward him, the camera jiggling all the way, but Abramov was clear and in focus in the center of the shot.

"This is right about where we lost the signal," Ali said.

Fatima felt her stomach tighten and her mouth go dry as she watched the camera movement stop when she reached Abramov. He loomed in the shot, his back still to her. Even on the monitor he seemed larger than life as he stood there. And stood there. And stood there. Never turning around. Never facing her. Never talking to her.

The sound of glass shattering came from the monitor, startling Fatima and Ali. The camera view swung around as a server rushed up and started cleaning up broken shards of a wine glass. It was Fatima's wine glass, which had slipped from her hand. The server asked if she'd like another glass of wine. She declined and hurried away.

Fatima was perplexed and feeling dizzy. *That's not what happened!*

Ali stopped and closed out the computer file. He stared at Fatima, not sure what to say.

"I know what I saw and heard. Abramov talked to me!" She hugged herself, feeling a chill run over her body. She sank into a nearby chair as if seeking protection in its overstuffed arms. "It wasn't a dream. It was real." *Or was it?*

CHAPTER EIGHT

Richard Abramov – the Dajjal – stood in a magnificent room on the top floor of his palace. The room was plush and comfortable and doubled as an office, a sanctuary, and what one might even refer to as a control room, with one wall filled with monitors, electronics, and computer equipment.

It also had shelves and glass cabinets filled with artifacts spanning several millennia. Priceless statues, trinkets, and weapons. Museum curators would salivate if they could lay eyes on what Richard had in his possession. They would be astounded that one man could have acquired such items, collected from all parts of the world from the dawn of history. And they would chuckle if he ever told them he personally had collected each and every treasure himself. He took statues after they were freshly created, new and pristine, though some were removed from the rubble of collapsed empires. Most of the weapons were taken from bloody battlefields shortly after being forged. The curators would laugh if he told them these stories and say, "Richard, you have such an imagination."

But each of those stories would be true.

Richard stood before the floor to ceiling windows that made up one entire wall and watched his guests depart the party. He stood in total darkness so if they happened to glance up, they wouldn't see him.

Darkness. He loved it. Possibly the only thing he loved. He was created in darkness. And it was a darkness so black there are no words to adequately describe it. Complete and total absence of light comes closest. Maybe.

He turned away from the window as his mind turned to the viral video footage he saw on the tabloid television show earlier in the evening. By now, likely the majority of the audience who caught that clip had forgotten about it and returned to their mundane lives filled with meaningless distractions. He knew a few religious fanatics would believe what they saw and focus on what was coming, but invariably they would be wrong. A few religious scholars might take note and pore through their ancient and dusty texts looking for answers.

But the Dajjal knew what he saw was real. And now he knew the rumors which had been floating around for centuries were true, and that he'd been deceived by what he witnessed two thousand years ago on the mountaintop called Golgotha – Place of the Skull.

He thought back to the series of events he followed and interfered with, way back then...

✳   ✳   ✳

The bearded man trudged up a hill and looked through thick foliage at a small, but nice house built on the outskirts of

Nazareth in Galilee. He felt compelled to come here and he knew never to resist that urge. That drive always led to important and necessary work.

He was dressed in the garments of the day – preferring a black tunic and gold belt most of the time – but seemed not so much to be one of the villagers. His leather sandals were not worn like those of most men, nor were his hands calloused. If he had lived in the region, where many of the adult men labored in the fields, he would have also stood with stooped shoulders, especially at his age. Instead, his posture seemed regal and commanding, though he wore not the dressings of royalty.

Looking through the thick brush, the bearded man – who wasn't going by any particular name now, although in two thousand years he would be called Richard Abramov, but who the angels always knew as the Dajjal – spied an elderly man, his equally elderly wife, a boy-child, and a pregnant teen girl sitting on a few benches in the garden, enjoying the day. Seemed normal enough, but he knew something important involving these people was coming, or else he wouldn't have followed the instincts that brought him here.

He moved away from the foliage and into the village and mingled with the residents. He asked around and quickly learned the elderly couple were Zakariya and his wife, Elizabeth. The infant boy was their child Yahya, and the pregnant teen girl was Maryam, their niece.

Not knowing how long he might need to be here, the bearded man set up shop as a blacksmith named Jacob. The shop was only a mile from Zakariya's house, close enough to easily follow whatever transpired with the small family.

It wasn't long before he heard the rumors spreading through the village. Stories of the Archangel Gabriel, sent by Allah, to bestow a child unto Maryam were on everyone's lips. A child with no earthly father.

"Your son will be a sign to the people and a miracle from Allah," Gabriel said to Maryam. Or so she claimed.

There were many who scoffed and dismissed the stories as the overactive imagination of a silly teenage girl. There were others who believed it.

But the bearded man *knew* it was true.

And nine months later a child was born.

A few days before the birth, Maryam announced to her aunt and uncle that she must go into the desert on a camel with few provisions since the Lord would take care of her. Zakariya was worried this was a mistake, and Elizabeth wept with fear over the dangers of experiencing childbirth alone. But Maryam insisted, and they saw her off. Her final instructions were for them to meet her on Mount Mariah in three days.

The bearded man attempted to follow her but inexplicably couldn't. That wasn't the first time he'd been prevented from a course of action. It didn't happen often, but he always knew it was the work of his enemy when it did. So, he patiently waited along with everyone else in the village.

The day came and a crowd gathered at Mount Moriah to await Maryam's return. The bearded man stood in the back of the crowd, quietly waiting, and observing.

The camel carrying Maryam and her newborn son soon emerged from the desert and stood in front of the people gathered there. Maryam smiled brightly and held the baby tight against her chest. Only the crown of his head was visible, adorned with a gentle cascade of soft, dark, curly hair. Maryam's eyes shone with kindness as she looked over the crowd, her gaze landing on the faces of her aunt and uncle.

A group of men helped Maryam dismount from the camel, and she walked to the front of the crowd, raising the child in the air.

"The Lord has told me to name him Isa," Maryam said.

Soon, from out of nowhere but the heavens, a man's voice sounded.

"I am the servant of God," the crowd heard. They were astonished. Some cowered and turned away. The voice seemed to come from the baby, but his mouth was not moving.

"He has given me the Scripture and made me a prophet. He has made me blessed wherever I am and has enjoined upon me prayer and zakah."

No one said anything but paid close attention to the words.

"I shall be dutiful to my mother. And peace is on me the day I was born and the day I will be raised alive," the voice concluded.

The people in the crowd all kneeled down in silent prayer, surrounding Maryam and the child. Zakariya and Elizabeth stood behind the new mother, heads bowed with hands raised in worship. All was silent but for the peaceful wind that blew through the gathering.

The bearded man slipped behind a large oak tree as all others knelt. He kneeled for none, save the source of his power, which was the being in the darkness, the one he'd never actually seen, nor had the desire to if he was honest with himself.

Though he'd moved through the world for thousands of years with nary a worry, this moment was different than all the moments that preceded it, and the bearded man was very troubled by the scene taking place before him, unsettled by what it meant. *This baby Isa…I must find a way to get rid of him.*

The bearded man followed Isa and his family over the coming years. He always stayed in the distance, blending in with the villagers, always just out of sight.

When Isa was 12 years old, the bearded man followed the little family to Jerusalem for Passover. After the Passover ceremony and celebration, Isa became separated from his mother and the others as they browsed the marketplace tents. Isa had no interest in such things and returned to the temple. The bearded man slipped in behind him and moved to the back of the crowd.

Though the Passover sermon had ended, there were men who wanted to discuss the Torah Scriptures for a bit longer. Isa was intrigued by the scholarly discussion, with his thirst for knowledge and the way of God.

The rabbi stood before the seated crowd. He wore gold rings on his fingers, fine linen cloth, and a bejeweled headdress, fitting for his role as the leader. "The temple is a place for God to abide. In the last chapter of Exodus, we are charged with a holy purpose, to create a home for God to inhabit."

Isa, deep in thought, raised his hand to ask a question. "What if one is unable to make it to the temple?" Isa asked with deep curiosity.

The men all turned to look at who was so bold to question the leader.

"Isn't God powerful enough to hear their prayers anywhere? Isn't He in our hearts? No matter where we are?"

Isa had the full attention of the crowd.

"What is your name, young man?" the leader asked impatiently.

"Isa." He stood humbly and tried his best to show respect to the man.

"This is God's house, Isa. It is His desire that all should commune with Him here."

"Then why do the temple authorities keep the poor out? Is it because they cannot tithe?"

The seated men all gasped, murmuring amongst themselves. The temple leader took a step closer to where Isa stood.

"There are rules. For one to attend…"

Isa interrupted him. "Man's rules. Not God's."

Awe and an air of discomfort flowed through the crowd. They were amazed at this boy who challenged the authority figure, a leader and priest. But not the bearded man. He was amused and entertained as he watched the exchange.

"There should be no rules – no restrictions – on reaching God," Isa continued.

Many men in the crowd nodded in agreement. A look of anger and frustration was apparent on the temple leader's face.

He glared at Isa and was about to say something when Maryam and Zakariya entered the temple.

"Isa, we were looking for you!" his mother said. "Why are you here?"

"But Mother, you should have known I would be in God's house," Isa replied.

"We must go now," Maryam said, motioning for Isa to come to her.

Isa nodded in obedience, stepped from the circle of men, and walked over to his mother and great-uncle.

"Isa!" The temple leader shouted. He wanted one last comment.

Isa and his mother turned to face the rabbi. Zakariya stood off to the side.

"You question where God abides, yet refer to the temple as God's house," he said smugly, his arms crossed in front of his chest.

Isa smiled warmly, radiating a peace that all could see. He shrugged his shoulders and stretched out his arms. "A house is not a prison. We can still travel where we choose. As can God."

At that, the leader's face reddened with more anger as he turned his back toward Isa.

Off to the side stood the bearded man. He enjoyed the exchange between the boy and the temple leader. Not for its knowledge. Not for its wisdom. But for the seeds of discontent and anger it sowed. He smiled with gritted teeth, a wicked and cunning smile.

Twenty years had passed since Isa had challenged the rabbi in the temple. Over time, word had spread about his wisdom, and many came to Jerusalem to hear Isa preach about God, his love and expectations of mankind. His cousin, Yahya, was also revered by many who came to listen to him at the banks of the Jordan River and talk of the faith of their ancestors. Throughout all this, the bearded man was ever present, always at the edge of the crowd, always observing, always patient, but never aging.

Still going by the name Jacob, he overheard that Yahya was frustrated and complained to Isa. Yahya told him that people were confused and expected him to baptize them with water unto Allah. Isa instructed him to tell them all are born unto a single creator and baptism is unnecessary. Yahya did just that, but many remained confused. Isa calmed his cousin, telling him to be patient. He was certain that in time people would learn.

Though Yahya preferred to preach outside the cities in Palestine, at times he was compelled to talk to the crowds in the marketplaces where they gathered.

On one such day, a man named Theodor made his way to the front of the crowd. He was adorned with fine jewelry and dressed in elaborate silk. He appeared to be in his fifties. Not far behind him stood the bearded man, curiously watching Theodor. When Yahya concluded his talk, Theodor approached him.

"I am Theodor, with the Herodian Dynasty. I've noticed your ministry has grown substantially in the short time you've preached in Palestine."

"It is God's doing, not mine," Yahya explained. "I am merely his servant."

The bearded man stood far off to the side where no one seemed to notice him. However, Isa took heed of him as he listened to the conversation taking place. Isa noticed all things.

"I suggest you would enjoy an audience with King Herod Antipas himself – what do you say to that?" Theodor's tone was calm but presented a challenge to Yahya.

Those from the crowd who had stayed stepped closer to hear what Yahya would say.

Yahya was indignant at the suggestion. "King Herod has divorced his wife and plans to marry the wife of his brother. That goes against all that is right and written in scripture! It is abominable in God's eyes!"

Theodor was unsure how to respond to Yahya's accusation and walked away.

Herod Antipas, a man of wealth and power, while seeming benevolent to his countrymen, was in reality a tyrant.

"What did Yahya say when you invited him to come see me?" Herod Antipas asked Theodor, who had just returned from seeing Yahya.

Theodor stood silent for a moment his head bowed. "He condemned your actions of divorce, and your plans to marry your brother's wife upon their divorce. He says it is against God's law."

Herod rose from his gilded chair and stomped across the room, waving his arms in anger. "These Jews and their laws – I am their ruler! I can do as I desire! I will marry Salome!"

The following week, Herod called for a celebration. It was held at night in his throne room, and many guests were present. They ate rich foods, had much to drink, and shared loud laughter. Herod sat on his throne, regal but drunk. Theodor called for everyone's attention.

"A special treat tonight, for all of you, but in particular, for Herod Antipas! This is a woman known to all of us, and she especially wanted to perform for her soon-to-be husband.

I present to you – Salome!"

Theodor pulled back the silken curtain, and the woman, young and beautiful, emerged in a sheer flowing dress, jewels sparkling on her arms and ankles. She seductively danced around the room, bending and stretching, twirling and spinning, for a long time, dazzling all who watched her smooth, silky movements. At the end of the dance, Salome stopped, breathless, in front of Herod. He could stand it no more and reached out for her. His hug was firm and tight, and the guests all applauded.

"I will fulfill your every desire," he breathed heavily in her ear. He could smell her perfume and it made him lust after her even more. "Anything you want, just tell me."

The crowd went silent and listened as Salome tilted her head back and laughed. Then she leaned in close and said in her most seductive voice, "Yahya has defiled our honor throughout the land. I want his head…on a platter. Grant me this wish as you make me your wife."

The people in the room all gasped at her request.

Herod embraced Salome and agreed, despite the murmurs he heard from his guests. As she pulled away and bowed, Herod noticed a bearded man standing in the shadows across the room. Though his face was darkened in the low light, Herod saw a broad smile on his face before the man disappeared. A cold breeze ruffled the curtain where the man had stood.

Herod blinked several times and shook his head. *The wine must be making me see things.*

The next morning, Herod dispatched a dozen Roman soldiers to collect Yahya. They found him preaching to a large crowd on the bank of the Jordan River. They dispersed the crowd and grabbed Yahya. He did not resist as they placed him on a horse and rode away.

The bearded man, who was part of the crowd, lingered as he watched with a grin Yahya disappearing in the dust created by the horse hooves.

Herod Antipas was pacing outside in his courtyard when the soldiers brought Yahya before him. The captain pulled Yahya off the saddle and ordered him to stand in front of Herod. The other soldiers formed a circle around the group. The captain pushed Yahya to his knees in front of a wooden box that lay on the ground.

"You have offended me! And my wife-to-be!" Herod shouted, spit spraying from his mouth.

"And you have offended God," Yahya said calmly. He did not falter in his stance.

Herod motioned to the captain, who then shoved Yahya forward, his neck bared on the wooden block. The captain raised his sword, waiting for the signal. Herod nodded, and the captain swung the sharp implement swiftly through Yahya's neck, smoothly slicing through flesh and bone. Yahya's bloody head rolled onto the dirt, and Herod turned away.

As he walked toward the palace door, he said loudly, "You know what to do with it."

Herod and Salome had finished eating dinner alone when he told her he had a gift for her. "I ordered it specially made for you," he said slyly.

"Really? I wonder what that could be, my dear? Another diamond bracelet? Perhaps a new outfit in which I may dance for you?" she said, laughing, as she laid back on the large white pillow placed behind her.

Herod snapped his fingers, and the captain of his soldiers strode in carrying a large silver platter with a domed lid.

"Oh, Herod, I have eaten enough. No more food, please!" She raised her hand as if to push away the platter.

"This is something that is sure to fill your senses, not your stomach," he laughed.

Herod motioned to the captain to come closer. He stood in front of Salome and raised the lid to reveal the bloody head of Yahya to her.

Salome smiled and shrugged, not shocked at the sight. She took a sip of wine. "My darling, this marks our new beginning," she said lovingly, raising her glass in a toast to Herod.

Herod returned the toast, his gaze filled with adoration.

The bearded man watched with satisfaction from the corner of the room. "Now just one more left," he whispered to himself, and disappeared.

Isa and Maryam were broken-hearted at the death of Yahya. But Isa knew there was much work to be done. More so, now that the burden had fallen squarely on Isa's shoulders, and his alone. He knew exactly what he needed to do.

Isa arrived at the temple early in the morning. He dismounted from his horse, tied it to a post, and entered.

Keeping a respectable distance, the bearded man followed Isa into the temple, carefully sticking to the shadows behind the gathering.

A sermon was in progress when Isa walked into the main hall. The rabbi was an elderly man with gray hair. He read from the Torah, his eyes squinting to see the words on the ancient pages. Isa walked with purpose up the center aisle and spoke in a loud, confident voice for all to hear.

"I come unto you with a sign from your Lord." All eyes fell on Isa as he approached the rabbi. "I fashion for you out of clay the likeness of a bird, and I breathe into it, and it is a bird by God's leave."

The temple leader contained his anger, but it was evident on his face.

Isa walked closer to where the leader stood. "I heal him who was born blind, and the leper, and I raise the dead, by God's leave," Isa said.

The gasps from the congregation were audible. Was this not blasphemy? The bearded man quietly watched from the shadows, like a theater patron attending a play.

"And I come confirming that which was before me of the Torah, and to make lawful some of that which was forbidden unto you," Isa continued, as he walked past the rabbi up the marble steps and faced the congregation. "I come unto you with a sign from your Lord, so keep your duty to God and obey me. God is my Lord and your Lord, so worship him. That is a straight path, a righteous one, and what God expects from everyone."

Some of the men in the seats nodded, some looked confused, and others appeared angry. The temple leader noticed something familiar about Isa.

"What is your name, young man?" the rabbi asked with a troubled look.

"My name is Isa." His warm smile disarmed the rabbi, who took a step back. The rabbi stood silent and shaken.

Leaving the temple, Isa walked a short distance and stopped at the corner of an intersection. He spoke in a loud voice, not offensive, but with compassion and kindness, to the people nearby. "I have come to attest to the Law which was before me. Who will be my helpers for the work of God? There is much to be done, and I ask for those of you called by God to accompany me. We will do the work of our Lord."

Isa caught the gaze of the bearded man who stood in the middle of the crowd. The two locked eyes and smiled briefly at one another before the bearded man's look turned to a scowl.

"Who will join me in my work spreading the word of God?" Isa asked.

A few men stepped forward. Isa greeted each with a warm hug and thanked them.

"You are willing to leave your homes and walk with me, not knowing what lies ahead?" he asked. They each nodded yes. Isa was pleased, and asked the crowd again, "Are there any others who are called to join me?

By the time all had come forward, there were eleven in number. Called from those who had listened for months to his message, they were willing to give up their homes and lives to tell others that Isa was the Messiah they had learned of through the ages.

"I will call you my apostles," he said. "Is there anyone else?"

Isa saw a man walking up from the side of the crowd. He looked much like the others in his robe and sandals, long hair tucked beneath a head wrap.

"What is your name, young man?" Isa asked.

"I am Judas Iscariot," he said. "I will be one of your apostles."

Isa shook his hand and gave him a hug. "Welcome, Judas."

In the following weeks and months, the apostles witnessed many miracles of healing that Isa performed, and each time, they were amazed at his powers. Isa laid hands on a crippled woman who had been unable to walk and healed her. He raised another woman's son from the dead after he had been buried in the ground. A leper approached him as they gathered at the river, and Isa cured his age-old, ugly skin disease, one that had resulted in him being banished from his family. He raised a young girl from death after she had fallen ill at her parents' house. He healed the crooked limbs of a man on a stretcher after his friends had lowered him through a hole in the roof in the house where Isa was preaching; the man was able to get up and walk for the first time since childhood.

On one of those miraculous days, Isa and the apostles walked to the top of the hillside, with many of the people following behind. A few feet away, some men argued about his teachings. His apostle Peter went to investigate and learned that they had questions about who Isa was.

"What is it, Peter?" Isa saw the men watching him from a distance.

"There are those who say you are the son of God. That your miracles prove it. Is it true?" he asked.

Isa sighed and assembled the crowd before him.

"I am a servant of God," Isa began. "He has given me revelation and made me a prophet. I am the messenger of God sent to you, confirming the words from the Torah about the Messiah, who I am, and I give glad tidings of a messenger to come in the years later, after me."

In the distance, the bearded man listened to what Isa had to say. Though far away, he heard Isa's words clearly. *God sent him? And he talks of another messenger? Isa does not know what havoc I can create, now and in later years. He will see.* With that, the bearded man walked away toward the desert and disappeared.

When Isa and his twelve disciples were not teaching the crowds, they withdrew in privacy to the outskirts of town and spent time in prayer and contemplation. As Isa stepped away from the others for a contemplative moment, Judas used the opportunity to approach him.

"Isa, you teach of love and compassion but is it not important for Israel to be free of Roman occupation? You have a formidable following. People would do anything for you if you just asked. When it comes to being freed from Roman rule, they would rise up in insurrection."

"The earthly affairs of men and their governments are not our concern," Isa said to Judas. "We should only focus on the desires of God. Nothing more. God's message is that of love, not anger. Not insurrection. Not hate and wars. It is not my intention to orchestrate any kind of war or instigate fighting. Do you see?"

Judas nodded but did not agree. He was troubled but willing to bide his time.

The pair returned to the circle where the others slept. Isa found a comfortable space to unroll his blankets and lie down as did Judas. After a time, all thirteen men were asleep.

Dreams overtook Isa's mind. He turned restlessly beneath his covers as he wrestled with the images that filled his head. He experienced himself walking to the edge of a very high cliff. A bearded man emerged from the darkness. Tall buildings appeared made of stone, metal, and glass, reaching to unimaginable heights. Metal, winged machines flew through the skies, and people communicated with each other instantly through rectangular handheld devices and through other glowing screens of assorted sizes. The bearded man waved his arm as if he were a magician.

"All these things I will give you if you fall down and worship me," he said.

Isa bolted awake and looked around. The others slept peacefully.

"No, that I will not do," he said firmly, staring up at the stars in the sky.

The following week, the leaders and rabbis gathered at the temple for a private meeting. "The Romans have agreed to assist us in eliminating Isa!" the temple leader explained joyfully. With Isa's ever-growing influence amongst the faithful, the rabbis feared an insurrection and sought Roman help in squelching it before it occurred.

A rabbi pushed his way to the front and stood before the temple leader. "Even so, it will be difficult. His following has grown to massive numbers. And he apparently performs miracles."

"What if they aren't miracles?" a voice boomed from the shadows. "What if Isa's miracles are only sorcery, a tool of Satan?"

The men gasped at the accusation as the bearded man emerged from the darkness. The temple leader moved closer to the bearded man, who stood about six inches taller than the leader.

"Who are you?"

"Just someone who wants to help," the bearded man said.

"Some say Isa is the Messiah!" one priest shouted.

"Nonsense! We would recognize him as such if it were true!" another chimed in.

The shouting increased as the men tried to talk over each other in a frenzy, to get their points across.

"There are some who claim he's the son of God," the bearded man said, his words plunging the room into silence.

The bearded man stepped closer to the group, continuing, "That's blasphemy. Sorcery and blasphemy are crimes."

The temple leader smiled. "Yes, we can have him tried on those charges! Then have him executed as the Romans suggested. Crucified!"

All the men exchanged glances with faces taut with tension. The gruesomeness of crucifixion was a ritual most temple priests avoided. So barbaric. So awful, a tortuous death, it seemed beyond anything humans should have to endure.

As they quietly talked among themselves, the bearded man turned away and quietly disappeared into the shadows from where he had come.

That evening, the temple leader, priests, and the people gathered for Passover. As the crowds entered the temple, the priests greeted each one, calling them by name, smiling. Judas was among those entering the building.

Judas requested to see the temple leader and a priest led him inside. The two men conversed quietly in the corner. The bearded man was on the opposite side of the room, feigning participation in the Passover ceremony as he listened to their conversation.

His sardonic grin split his face as he overheard Judas angrily betray Isa. Judas claimed Isa was going to have his followers move against the Roman occupation during Passover. The bearded man knew Judas was lying. He couldn't tell if the temple leader believed him or not, but it was a moot point. The leader was looking for any excuse to act against Isa and now he had one.

When the temple leader asked Judas where Isa could be found, Judas requested thirty pieces of silver for the information. The temple leader was taken aback but Judas was steadfast in demanding payment. "Who else would do this for you?" Judas asked.

The temple leader nodded and summoned an assistant to bring the silver coins in a pouch. After the handoff, Judas gave the man the information he sought.

"Isa is at the Cenacle on Mount Zion. Give me about an hour so that dinner will be complete before you and the Roman soldiers convene. He won't suspect what's coming."

The temple leader nodded and shook Judas's hand before he took leave.

Across the room, the bearded man stood and walked out of the temple. He didn't want to miss what was coming for the world. That meant he would have to change his normal role in this situation – become a new character. Tonight, he will not be Jacob the blacksmith; he will be Jacob the Roman soldier.

Later that evening, the bearded man, wearing traditional Roman soldier garb, rode hard on horseback with twenty other soldiers toward Mount Zion. None of the other soldiers questioned his sudden presence. Roman soldiers were reassigned on a regular basis; they knew it was not unusual. He had a sword strapped to his side, but he knew he couldn't directly interfere with what was about to occur. As usual, he would hang back and let the other soldiers do the dirty work. The bearded man would, yet again, become an observer to history. A history he helped facilitate.

As Mount Zion loomed before them, something caught the bearded man's attention. He glimpsed a bright ball of light suddenly emerging from the other side of the mountain and quickly disappearing into the clouds. The soldiers surrounding him didn't seem to notice. If the bearded man were human, he would've thought he imagined it. But the only thing human about him was his appearance. Nothing more. He was not prone to hallucinations or fanciful imaginings. No. Whatever this sphere of light was, it was certainly real.

He and the Roman soldiers worked their way up the side of the mountain to the Cenacle. He heard a commotion coming from inside as they closed in on the structure.

"What is wrong, Isa?" the bearded man heard an apostle ask.

"I'm not Isa. I am Judas Iscariot!" Isa screamed at them with panic in his voice.

The bearded man looked around and wasn't surprised the other soldiers heard nothing as they all stampeded toward the

Cenacle. He was a bit confused at Isa's state of mind, however. This so-called Messiah didn't seem to be one easily given into fear. But, then again, regardless of the virgin birth, the alleged miracles and resurrections, Isa was still simply a frail human being, unlike the bearded man.

The companions stared at Isa in confusion and concern as the Roman soldiers rode their horse into the midst of the group and quickly dismounted. They headed for Isa. The bearded man hung back and observed. Something about Isa's behavior was odd. He appeared in every way to be Isa – his features, his build, his clothing was correct. But his demeanor was all wrong.

"Isa, you are under arrest for insurrection against Rome!" the captain said. "Grab him!"

Isa turned to run away, but the soldiers moved on him quickly. They knocked him to the ground and bound his hands behind his back. Isa struggled, kicking, and flailing about.

Isa screamed. "No! You have the wrong man! I am not Isa…I am Judas Iscariot!" His face and lips bled as he fought hard to free himself.

"Arrest them all!" the captain shouted, and the soldiers obeyed, taking the men into custody.

The bearded man slipped further into the darkness of shadows and watched. Despite the odd actions and conduct of Isa, he enjoyed watching the chaotic scene. He always enjoyed such things as far back as he could remember. Thousands of years at this point. He was pleased with what was happening.

As Isa and his companions were hauled off, the bearded man realized that Judas Iscariot was not accounted for. The man whom Isa claimed to be was simply gone. The bearded man was perplexed for only a moment before chuckling.

Judas knew this was coming so he obviously made his getaway. Smart man.

Showing a wide grin, the bearded man strolled down a dirt path and disappeared.

A trial before Pontius Pilate was scheduled for the following morning. Isa was charged with many crimes against the Romans and the Jews. Nonetheless, Pilate declared publicly that he found Isa to be innocent of the charges. But the crowd yelled, "Crucify him!" "He deserves to die!" "He has broken our laws!"

Pilate shook his head, amazed at the anger of the Jews. He asked his aides for a bowl of water and a towel. "I hear nothing that is worthy of killing this man," he said as he washed his hands to absolve himself from any conviction. "He is yours to deal with," he said and walked back into the palatial complex.

The bearded man hovered at the back of the proceedings and followed Isa as he was taken away by the Roman soldiers to be whipped and his head pierced with a crown of thorns. He was pleased at the look of panic and fear on Isa's face. As the group disappeared, he was sure he heard Isa again say, "My name is Judas Iscariot." *Perhaps this man had indeed gone crazy.*

The sun rose high in the sky, casting short shadows on the valley's fields. Far off in the distance, at the top of a hill outside the city, hundreds of people lined the path that led to the top of the mountain. Row after row of men and women stood on both sides of the path, at least four people deep. Everyone shouted. Some threw stones. Others wept. The crack of a whip hitting human flesh rose above the shouts and weeping. Vultures rested on tree limbs near the execution site. A dark weather front hung in the distance.

Coming up the path dragging his cross was Isa. He had been beaten horribly, nearly beyond recognition, his face dripped with sweat and blood. His clothing was dirty, and his long hair and beard matted. The pained look on his face was agonizing to those who saw him. The heavy wooden cross laid over his shoulder dug into his skin, and he was bent from the weight of it, dragging its end in the dirt. The Roman soldiers were stern and pushed him if he hesitated, even for a moment.

Some shouted to crucify him, that he was a criminal. Others pleaded for his life, saying he was the Messiah, and a prophet of God. Isa's mother, Maryam, screamed in anguish at what was happening to her son. She was so overcome with pain and despair at the sight of him, she collapsed as he trudged past her showing no sign of recognition.

The Roman soldiers cracked their whips, driving Isa to the top of the hill toward the large, wooden cross that awaited him.

Out of sight of the crowd, the bearded man watched with interest. A sly smile was on his face, and he nodded slowly, stroking his beard.

"What a wonderful day," he said softly to himself as he gleefully watched. With that, he followed the route where Isa was heading, to the mountaintop called Golgotha – Place of the Skull – to triumphantly witness the life fade from Isa.

*   *   *

Richard Abramov watched the last of his guests driven away in a limousine. Another successful party had ended but he was troubled. For centuries he'd heard rumors that Isa avoided his dire fate by praying to Allah, who responded by lifting him up – alive – into Heaven. The rumors said, following that, Judas Iscariot's appearance was transfigured into Isa. He was then substituted for Isa at the crucifixion.

Though it all added up – witnessing the glowing sphere rising into the clouds and Isa's uncharacteristic behavior, claiming to be Judas – it just seemed so unbelievable to the Dajjal. So, he pushed it out of his mind. Denied it. That thought alone unnerved the Dajjal. It was so human. Something he didn't want to consider he could fall victim to.

Nonetheless, it appears that's exactly what happened. And now it appears that Isa has returned to Earth. No problem. I've dealt with him before and removed him from the picture. And kept him out of it for two thousand years. I can do it again. For another two thousand years. Or longer since he's a flesh-and-blood human. Maybe this time I can get rid of him forever.

A confident smile crossed his face as his eyes turned black as coal.

CHAPTER NINE

The next morning, Fatima and Ali met for breakfast in the hotel restaurant. The place was nearly empty, which surprised no one. The hotel was usually filled with businesspeople and vacationers, but after the terrorist attacks on the Holy Sites, most people were understandably cutting their trips short. And even though Israel hadn't lifted its flight ban yet, people were finding other ways to get out of the country. Some took boats to neighboring countries and flew from there. Others took cars. These trips created their own challenges, as this entire region of the world had a tendency to be more dangerous to travelers.

Fatima and Ali weren't leaving, nor had they ever intended to. And now, they practically had the restaurant to themselves. They sat in a corner booth for privacy though it didn't matter. Ali picked his way through a bowl of fruit and a glass of orange juice as Fatima nibbled at a piece of toast and nursed a cup of coffee. He looked well-rested – Fatima, not so much.

Ali stopped eating and watched Fatima with curiosity. He was subtle about it, but not subtle enough. Or maybe Fatima was just that astute of an observer. Either way, the way he looked at her made her uncomfortable.

"What are you thinking, Ali?"

Ali sat back in the booth and gathered his thoughts. "I was just thinking back to what you told me last night. That Abramov said something like, 'You're right, I have read all the holy books.'"

"That's exactly what he said," she confirmed.

"What do you think he was referring to?" he asked with faux innocence.

"Don't mess with me," she snapped back. "You know what he meant."

Ali slowly nodded, unflapped at her annoyance. The waitress wandered over with a pot of coffee. Fatima covered her cup with the palm of her hand. Ali smiled and nodded at the waitress who proceeded to top off his cup. He waited until the waitress had walked away before continuing.

"Yes, I know what he meant," he said, lowering his voice. "He was referencing the reason you said the Dajjal didn't exist."

She nodded, embarrassed, but with a tinge of fear. *How could he know the private conversation I had with Ali days earlier? Does he know everything we do and discuss?*

"I can only come to two conclusions about this," Ali said after taking a sip from his steaming coffee cup.

"Okay," she said with trepidation as she eagerly waited for him to continue.

"You either imagined the entire thing with your mind using the information from our conversation. Kind of how we influence our own dreams. Or…"

"Well?" she asked as she clutched her coffee cup for support.

"Or it's real. He is the Dajjal," he said matter-of-factly as he took a drink of coffee.

She rolled her eyes. "I'm sorry, Ali, I just can't go there." *I'm stuck in denial but can't tell you that. Maybe, after I work it out in my own mind, we can discuss it openly.*

"Then what do you think happened?"

"I don't know." She stood, clearly done with the conversation. At least for now. "I'm going up to my room and chill for a while. Figure out what we need to do next."

"Okay," he said with a nod. "I'll catch up with you later."

She turned and walked away, leaving Ali alone to finish his breakfast, and contemplate the implications of Richard Abramov possibly being the Dajjal.

*   *   *

In the secured offices of his mansion, the Dajjal seethed, worked into a frenzy as he watched television show clips he'd culled from the internet. He viewed them on multiple windows splashed across the massive flatscreen that practically filled one wall of his office. There were images of various quality and angles depicting the "man coming from the sky" from the night before, during his party, when he had encountered Fatima Al-Hasan. He pushed thoughts of her out of his mind. She was insignificant. Someone he could deal with later, if he had to deal with her at all.

He focused on the news clips all playing simultaneously. The resulting cacophony of voices colliding together would have been beyond distracting to most, but Richard could decipher it all with ease. Speculation covered the entire gamut: Is it a hoax? An extraterrestrial? A trick of light and shadow? Or Jesus Himself?

But the Dajjal already knew Isa – or Jesus as the Christians and Jews called him – had returned. The world just hadn't quite gotten up-to-speed yet. With a flick of his remote, the large flatscreen went dark. Time to get down to real business.

He pushed buttons hidden in the shelf of a bookcase and the massive shelf swung open to the right, revealing his large control room filled with rows of computers, electronic maps of the world on the wall, along with screens that showed locations of missile silos and heavy military equipment. The Dajjal stepped inside and seated himself at a large, high-backed, leather chair that had controls in each armrest. He punched numbers into the control pad, and one by one, faces popped up onto 3D monitors that lined the wall before him. He had audio and video connections with various heads of state, public officials, and business owners. Many had been at the party Abramov held the night before. A flight ban wouldn't stop them from returning home. They all arrived and left on private jets which had landed on the airstrips on Abramov's property behind his palace.

When the Dajjal was ready to speak to them, he pushed another button that connected his microphone to the system.

"Hello, my dear friends." His voice was smooth and calm. "You have undoubtedly heard about the events at the Great Mosque in Damascus. Even though most of the world will dismiss it as nonsense, you and I know otherwise." Every person in view on the screens nodded in unison, as if hypnotized. "This is just the beginning. I will handle it. You will receive information via a highly classified email from me with the scripts I expect each of you to follow. All of you know what to do. Do not rely on news media reports nor are you to grant any interviews. I am the one person you are to listen to. Understand?"

All the heads nodded again. Dajjal pushed a button, and the screens went blank. For one brief moment, while completely alone, his features changed into something hideous. He fully became the Dajjal, nostrils flaring, black eyes flashing, before he snapped back to the façade of Richard Abramov.

*   *   *

Fatima was lying, fully clothed, on her hotel room bed as she stared at the ceiling. She wasn't tired, just thinking. *I went to a high-class party to gather intel on someone who might be responsible for the terrorist attack in Jerusalem and left with a paradigm shift on my views of the universe. Is it me, or the world that has gone crazy?*

A text from Ali drew her attention. "Come to my room. There's something I need to show you," was all it said. She grinned. Leave it to Ali to send a cryptic message.

A few minutes later, Fatima knocked on Ali's hotel room door. He cracked it open as if she was a spy, needing to give him the password.

"I'm here. What's up?" She was not having any part of his games today. He got the message loud and clear and opened the door with a smile on his face. He glanced up and down the hallway after she entered, then he closed it.

Ali led Fatima over to his workstation and plopped into the desk chair. Fatima stood behind him and looked over his shoulder. She picked up this habit working at *News World*. It was what all the station directors did in the control room. She toyed with being a news director someday, a few decades from now, when she either got bored being in front of the camera, or "aged out." The news business always preferred young faces on-screen. Particularly if they were female faces. Fatima didn't like it but knew it was the reality of working in the news industry. Thus, she subtly, and unconsciously, prepared for the day she would have to redirect her news career to other aspects of it.

Ali hit the space bar and a news clip started playing on his main monitor. It was apparently something he had already cued up before she arrived.

It was the same news clip with the perky announcer Richard Abramov saw on the television above the bar at his party. Fatima and Ali quietly watched the entire thing. The host squirmed with excitement as she talked, almost shouting, straight into the camera.

"Videoclips from a crowd gathered in Damascus have gone viral. It shows a man descending from the sky."

The image of the announcer was replaced by a grainy and shaky videoclip of a silhouetted man with his arms spread high in the air against a starry sky. As he got closer to the camera his features became clearer. He sported contemporary clothing with a yellow shirt and jeans. He also had a modern haircut and a well-groomed beard.

The energetic female announcer concluded with, "There are some who are saying this is Jesus...*the* Jesus Christ... returning to Earth." She smiled out at her audience with a freeze-frame of the man descending from the sky behind her.

Ali paused the clip with a tab of his space bar. "I cross-referenced it with video clips all over YouTube of the same event. If it were just one clip, I'd say some kid with a CGI program created it, but it can't be."

"Some kind of hoax maybe?" Fatima asked as she leaned in for a closer look at the frozen image on the monitor. "A publicity stunt of some sort?"

"Well, I guess that is a complete possibility, except for two things."

"Which are?"

"The destruction of the Dome of the Rock for one. Even you said that there were those who believed it signaled the End Times. At least from a Christian perspective."

"Yeah, that's right. But I'm not entirely convinced," Fatima said, her uncertain tone betraying her wavering belief. Ali tossed her a glance but didn't press the issue.

"You said *two* things. What's the other?" she asked, not sure she really wanted to know.

"Your encounter with Abramov last night."

Fatima suddenly straightened up and paced nervously back and forth, her agitation evident. Ali followed her with his gaze like someone watching a tennis match.

"Don't you think that's a bit of a coincidence?" he asked.

Fatima looked down and fidgeted with her hands. "I don't know what to think."

"Fine. Nothing wrong with that. We all need to figure things out for ourselves. But I know what we should do."

She stopped pacing and looked at him. "What?"

"Go to the Umayyad Mosque in Damascus."

She stared at him. "Are you crazy?"

Ali jumped to his feet with enough force to cause his chair to roll back and slam into his workstation. He didn't care, never so much as looked back. "Think about it, Fatima. It would make a great story. Something happened last night in Damascus. Maybe it is a hoax. You can be the news correspondent chasing the story." Ali gave her a satisfied smile, thinking that would clinch the deal.

But it didn't. She dismissed it out of hand. "I'm not a tabloid reporter, Ali. I'm a legitimate journalist. Christopher Munson would have to approve it, and he would think I'm crazy."

Ali stroked his beard as he tried to come up with a new angle for her. His eyes widened and a sly smile filled his features. "Fine. Then go there to get the Islamic perspective on the destruction of the Al-Aqsa Mosque and the Dome of the Rock. That's clearly newsworthy. And while you're there, you can interview this so-called Isa if he's even around anymore. You don't even have to tell Mr. Munson about that part."

Fatima nodded as she considered this new course of action. *Going into Syria will no doubt be dangerous. But would it be any more dangerous than being near ground zero during the terrorist attack on the Dome and the Al-Aqsa Mosque? And I would – hopefully – get a chance to meet this man that some think is Isa. It's ironic that I would even consider taking such a treacherous journey to learn if the very faith I rejected is true. I guess in its own way, that is a test of faith in and of itself.*

Fatima looked Ali right in the eyes. "Let's do it!" she said without hesitation. "I'll contact Christopher and get permission." She thought a moment. "Forget permission! I'll talk him into it."

Ali smiled so wide he looked like a cartoon character. "I'm confident you'll succeed."

He sat back down and looked at the frozen, grainy image on the monitor.

"Jesus to Jesus," he said softly to himself.

Fatima heard him. "What was that, Ali?"

"Just something from an interfaith conference I attended a few years ago in Chicago," he said as he swiveled to face her. "It was the title of one of the seminars being given. Jesus to Jesus. The speaker was a Muslim, but he used the more common name for Isa that most people in the United States used."

Fatima's curiosity was piqued. "What does that even mean – Jesus to Jesus?"

"In the context the speaker was using, he meant the two sides of Jesus, or Isa. See, Jesus is an important figure in both Christianity and Islam."

"I know that," Fatima said.

"In both religions, he is the Messiah. And although the Jews don't view him as the returning Messiah, they acknowledge him as a prophet that walked the Earth two thousand years ago. So, he's important in all three religions. At least one side of him is – the side that was the prophet. When he walked the Earth, his primary goal was to preach God's message and turn people to God. That's the first Jesus in the 'Jesus to Jesus' phrase."

"And the second part?"

"That's when he comes back as the Messiah. If that is indeed him, that is at the Great Mosque, he will be a somewhat different person than he was the first time he was here."

"In what way?"

"He's not here to preach, or to bring people to God. He's here as a fighter. To battle the Dajjal."

"How big a battle could something like that be?"

"Nobody really knows. It's just speculation at this point. It could be very small and personal, like two men in a boxing ring. Or maybe bigger."

"Like how big?" Fatima asked, letting her journalistic instincts take over when she didn't get a straight answer to a question the first time she asked it.

Ali shrugged. "I don't know. Big enough to wreck the world possibly."

Fatima shuddered at the thought, which surprised her. *Why did I react that way? I don't believe in any of this. It's nonsense. Or is it?*

It took Fatima a great deal longer to reach Christopher Munson than she had anticipated. The time difference between New York and Israel always seemed to strike at the most inconvenient, and annoying time. She left several messages for him over several hours. When he finally got back with her and they set up a fast Zoom call, he was more worried than aggravated at her persistence, thinking something disastrous may have happened to her or Ali. That worry dissolved into an angry glare once she told him why they needed to talk.

"Damascus?! That sounds a bit dangerous, Fatima."

"I know, but isn't that what correspondents do: go into dangerous areas?"

He sighed. She always did this to him. Stated the obvious while ignoring the equally obvious counterpoint. She went on before he could say anything. "And it's a perfect follow-up to the terrorist attacks in Jerusalem. Two Islamic holy sites destroyed. Getting the Muslim perspective from those at the Great Mosque of Damascus will be a great scoop."

Christopher was perplexed at her logic. "But wasn't the destruction most likely caused by TRIAD? And they are, well… mostly Muslims."

"They might have started out as Muslims, replacing extremists that came before them, like ISIS," she replied. "But now they are a mix of extremists from various religions, and even secularists."

"But TRIAD is behind the attacks, right?" Christopher asked, with a touch of frustration in his voice. He hated it when someone didn't give him a direct answer.

"Nobody knows that for sure," she said. Fatima was a lousy liar and her voice betrayed knowledge that she wasn't sharing. Christopher made a mental note of it but chose not to push the issue.

"You do know there are thousands of people traveling there, don't you?"

"No, I didn't actually," she said, genuinely surprised.

"Yeah, ever since the footage of the so-called Jesus descending from the sky above the mosque, crowds are headed there."

"I didn't hear about that," she said unconvincingly.

"You didn't? It was on a tabloid show," he said with a raised eyebrow and a trace of an accusatory tone.

Fatima rolled her eyes. "I don't watch those, Christopher. I'm a legitimate journalist."

He blushed with embarrassment. "Okay. I'll approve your expense for the Damascus trip." Then he pointed a finger at her with so much force she thought it was going to emerge from her computer screen. "But you and Ali be extra cautious."

"Always," Fatima said innocently before suddenly ending the call. She leaned back and sighed in relief as her laptop screen returned to her familiar desktop clutter. *I did it! We're going to Damascus. But we need to be on our toes. This isn't a vacation. Far from it!*

CHAPTER TEN

It was late morning after his palace party as the Dajjal stood by the window and looked straight into the sun without squinting or blinking. Though he would never admit it to anyone – even barely admitting it to himself – his encounter with Fatima Al-Hasan disturbed him. The world had changed so much over the millennia, particularly in the last few decades, he was slowly losing the battle with technology. His presence in the world was seeping through his control net. The fact that Fatima and her associates had punctured through his secretive veil, even briefly, told him that one day the world could soon be aware of his presence. But the Dajjal knew what he needed to do.

If you can't stop the narrative, then at least control the narrative, he thought.

"Okay… things have been set in motion; no stopping them now," he said to no one in particular. "Time to get on with it."

He summoned his limo to meet him out front of his palace. He didn't really need it. What no one knew was that Richard

Abramov could travel around the world at will in the blink of an eye. He only needed to take something as painfully slow as an automobile, or even a jet, for appearance's sake when he needed a public face. It would be alarming if one group of elites saw Abramov in New York in one moment, then another group saw him in Japan the next moment. People would talk, and that's never good.

He climbed into his limo and sat back in the cushioned leather seat, crossed his legs, and enjoyed a drink.

Destination: Downtown Jerusalem.

About a half-hour later, his black limousine pulled to a stop in front of one of the most prestigious hospitals in Jerusalem. A parking attendant wearing an orange reflective vest opened the door to the occupant in its back seat. A man dressed in a suit wearing a name badge that read "Jacob Katz, Administrator" walked quickly to greet the passenger as he stepped languidly out of the vehicle.

"Mr. Abramov, welcome," the nervous man said, extending a hand. His wire-rimmed glasses slipped down his sweaty nose, his underarms also drenched from the tension. Abramov shook Katz's hand as the limo drove off.

"Sir, we are honored for the generous financial gift you provided today for the victims of the mosque destruction," the administrator said. "It will ensure those without means will have the best possible care."

"I'm glad I could be of assistance," Abramov said. "Now, if I may, I would like to meet some of the victims."

"Yes, of course," Katz eagerly said.

Katz led Abramov to the main floor elevator. The pair rode in silence to the fourth floor, where the administrator introduced Abramov to the nursing staff, who had been alerted in advance of the important man's arrival.

Katz told them Abramov would like to see some of the victims. The head nurse led them to a room where an elderly man lay unconscious in the bed, a spider-web of tubes and wires crisscrossing his body. Machines off to the side beeped while their electronic graphs tracked his breathing, heart rate, and blood pressure.

In a chair to the patient's left sat a younger man whose resemblance to the elder indicated he was the man's son. He stood at once when Abramov and Katz entered the room. He bowed as he wiped tears away.

"This is Sadeem," Katz said. "He is mute. His father is Talib. We are trying to locate a person skilled in signing, so we can communicate with Sadeem."

As if on cue, Abramov began to form signs with his hands directed at the young man. He whispered the words, so the others could understand. It was apparent to all present that Sadeem understood what Abramov communicated. A big smile broke out on the son's face.

"I'm very sorry about your father. I'm here to help in any way I can," Abramov signed.

Sadeem's hands flew back and forth, shaping words directed at Abramov. A look of relief shone on his face. He shed more tears but this time he was smiling.

"My prayers are with you and your family," Abramov concluded, putting an arm around the young man's shoulder.

Without warning, the heart monitor flat-lined and the beep held steady in a continuous tone. One nurse called for a "code blue" and two technicians rushed in with a cart full of equipment and medical supplies. They surrounded Talib as the son and the others backed away.

"We should step out of the room," Katz told them, turning toward the door.

Abramov instead stepped closer to the patient's bed and touched the man on his forehead with one hand. He closed his eyes and was quiet.

The others watched in surprise, not sure what to say or do as the tone from the heart monitor stayed steady. The technicians pulled out the paddles but before they placed them on Talib's chest, regular beeps sounded, and a jagged line appeared on the screen as Abramov held his hand steady against the man's forehead. Then he stroked the man's face and his eyes fluttered open. Talib looked around for his son, as the nurses and technicians stood silent at the foot of the bed, their mouths open.

Sadeem, still mute but filled with surprise, looked from his father to Abramov, and back again. He was happy his father was still alive. However, something about Abramov caused him to panic and he began to frantically make hand signs. It was obvious Sadeem was upset but no one could understand his words, which seemed angry by the intensity of his signing.

"What's he saying?" the administrator asked Abramov.

"I don't know. It's too fast," Abramov lied, standing next to Sadeem.

The young man tried to communicate with Katz and the others, but it was futile. In an instant, he leaped forward and grabbed Abramov by the throat. Abramov fought him off, grabbing the young man by both wrists. He pushed Sadeem back towards the wall.

"We need security! Now!" Katz yelled through the doorway. The others in the room came to Abramov's aid and held Sadeem. Two security guards entered the room and pulled Sadeem out into the hallway as he continued to struggle and glare at Abramov.

Katz was embarrassed and apologized to his benefactor. "I'm so sorry about this. I can have him arrested for what's he's done to you. I can't imagine what brought that on."

Abramov was gracious and calm. He rubbed his neck where he had been grabbed. "No need. Sadeem is simply upset and overwhelmed with emotion. His father nearly died. Is there a restroom nearby? I need to clean myself up if I may."

"Yes. Nurse, please show Mr. Abramov to a restroom," he said, and she obliged.

The security guards led Sadeem to the elevator and escorted him out the front door with a stern glare, a clear sign he was to stay away. As they went back inside, Sadeem searched for a side door to reenter the hospital. The first one was locked but a few feet away, two hospital employees exited from another. Sadeem smiled at them as they walked past him, then he grabbed the door before it closed. Creeping around the hallways and making sure security didn't see him, he took the elevator back up to the fourth floor.

He stepped out of the elevator just in time to see the nurse escorting Abramov to the men's room. She nervously gabbed, gushing all over him – a wealthy man who gave such a generous donation to the hospital – as she walked alongside him. For his part, Abramov looked bored and distracted. She was oblivious to it, but Sadeem wasn't. As Abramov disappeared into the restroom, Sadeem took out his mobile phone and activated the camera function. Taking a deep breath, he strode toward the restroom.

The men's restroom was empty, and Abramov quickly washed his face. He expressionlessly viewed himself in the mirror. He didn't care about the victims of the bombings. Not at all. He was here simply to plant the seeds for what was to come next. The world was about to be awakened. And he wanted to be sure he could persuade as many as possible – hundreds of millions, or maybe a billion or two – that he was the good guy. Donating millions to a hospital was one way to get that train rolling.

He reached up and plucked out his right eyeball, which was made of glass. He stared at it with his one good eye, then gazed at his image in the bathroom mirror. Though he had been alive nearly forever he was still amazed at having lost an eye. It happened during the Battle of Awtas in 630 A.D.

Unlike Isa, who was a turn-the-other-cheek peacekeeper, Muhammad was a fighter who acted in self-defense when attacked. He also led successful campaigns throughout Arabia against those who threatened him and his followers.

The Dajjal, going by one of many names he used as the bearded man, tried repeatedly to have him killed. Though each attempt failed, he came within a hair's breadth when Muhammad came with 12,000 Muslim fighters to battle a coalition of tribes at Awtas. The Dajjal orchestrated an ambush by having the tribe's archers rain thousands of arrows down on the Muslims, with the heaviest concentration where Muhammad himself was camped.

The Dajjal wanted to bask in the glory of seeing God's last prophet die. This time in battle, his body peppered with arrows. He teleported close-by when the assault started early in the morning, to have a front-row view. As the Muslim fighters fled the onslaught, Muhammad and a few of his most loyal men stood their ground with shields raised above their heads.

Muhammad's attention was fully focused on the battle at hand, and he was unaware of the Dajjal's presence. The Dajjal grinned as he watched the onslaught of arrows on Muhammad's position. Eventually an arrow would fell Muhammad, and another prophet would be laid to rest.

Then the unexpected – and unthinkable – happened.

While struggling to keep his shield above his head, fighting against the ever-increasing weight of it as it collected arrows, Muhammad used his sword to deflect some arrows coming toward him at an oblique angle. One of those deflected arrows was absently and unintentionally knocked straight toward the Dajjal.

It pierced his right eye. For the first time since he came into existence, the Dajjal felt pain. Intense pain. He quickly teleported to an open desert and yanked the arrow from his eye, then shrieked in pain so loudly it echoed around the entire planet, turning the sand beneath him into glass for miles.

He thought the eye would reform, but it never did.

Though Muhammad escaped death that day, the bearded man claimed victory when Muhammad succumbed to death in Medina a few years later, on June 8, 632 A.D., after several painfilled days of illness. It was a hollow victory. Muhammad might be dead but his mark on the bearded man remained. For centuries afterward, he was "the bearded man with the eye patch" until modern medical technology supplied him with a glass eye so realistic most people never knew he only had one good eye.

The Dajjal had often pondered that long-gone day and wondered how Muhammad could have done that. *Was it just because he was a man of God*, the Dajjal mused? *Was anything and everything that came within his sphere of influence charged with some kind of spiritual power?*

Or was it something else entirely? The memory of losing his eye had always been unusually vague and fuzzy for the Dajjal. Every moment of his existence was crystal clear in his mind, except the moments leading up to, and after, he lost his eye. Those moments were illusory.

Was it just a dream? But how could it be? My eye is gone. I lost it somehow. If it didn't happen during Muhammad's battle, then how? Punishment from my father for some reason? From my Enemy for trying to influence the events surrounding one of his chosen?

These were questions he would never know the answers to, and he accepted that. Irrelevant anyway. It was a waste of time to contemplate on how things should've gone. Sure, he lost an eye – though not completely certain how – but Muhammad was dead and buried and that's all that mattered.

The Dajjal rolled the glass eye around in his fingertips, appreciating the workmanship. Humans were certainly good for some things, he thought.

He pulled a small bottle out of the inside breast pocket of his suit jacket and dropped a bit of the liquid on the orb. He was drying it with a paper towel as the restroom door pushed open and Sadeem snapped a photo of him with his cell phone camera. Sadeem quickly turned and left the restroom. The Dajjal carefully placed the glass eye back in its socket, and admired his reflection in the mirror, a wolfish grin on his face. He turned and marched fearlessly out into the hallway.

Outside, Sadeem hid in the shadows next to the door where he had gained reentry to the main floor. His hands shook as he pulled out two small books from his pants pockets. The first was the Qur'an. Quickly leafing through it, he was unable to find what he sought and shoved it back into his pocket. The second book contained Muslim Hadiths. He paged through it, searching, finally landing on the page he was looking for. He read silently to himself: *He will come to some people claiming to be Allah and they will believe him. Upon his order, the sky will rain, and the Earth will produce crops for these people...*

He flipped a few more pages and again read, *He will approach a Bedouin whose parents have passed away and will say to him, 'Will you believe that I am your Lord if I bring your parents back to life?'* He looked left and right, wide-eyed with fear, and breathed deeply to calm himself. Thrusting back his shoulders, he tucked the book away and rushed off down the sidewalk, now a man with a mission.

Abramov exited the front doors of the hospital, having said his goodbyes to Katz and his staff. The sun shone overhead, and he decided to walk instead of call for the limousine. A large crowd of people were in the vicinity of the hospital – some having just been discharged, waiting for rides; others getting out of vehicles, sitting in wheelchairs. Some were taken out of ambulances on stretchers and wheeled inside.

For secularists, humanitarian aid is what is needed. But for the religious, a more direct approach works better. A supernatural approach.

Nearby, a mother pushed a young girl in a wheelchair. She was hunched over from years of pushing the bulky unit, her eyes sad with worry. Abramov walked up to the pair and began talking to them. He asked about the girl's condition and expressed genuine concern. "How would you like to be able to walk again?" he asked the girl, bent down on one knee to be at her eye level.

The mother and daughter exchanged glances, both saying, "Yes! Of course. Who are you?"

"You shall see." Abramov touched the girl on her head as he closed his eyes for a minute. He opened them, stood, and stepped back a bit. He motioned for her to stand.

The young girl hesitated, then held herself steady on the wheelchair's arms while her mother supported the chair from behind. "I can stand!" she shouted with joy, as she rose from the seat. "Look at me!"

The mother wept and hugged her daughter. "It's a miracle! The doctors told us she would never regain the use of her legs!" The crowd who witnessed the scene clapped and cheered. Many pulled out cell phone cameras and began recording the scene as Abramov walked on.

Soon, videos of my miracles will be all over the internet, and the world will know. He smiled to himself, looking for similar opportunities – for it was his time to come out into the limelight, behind the scenes no more. *I have waited for this time when the world is connected by technology. From the comforts of home, work, in restaurants, or coffee houses, they will see me. They will know. And many will turn to me as planned through the ages.*

CHAPTER ELEVEN

Paul Sheppard strolled through the market in the heart of Damascus, watching a video on his tablet. Even though his eyes were focused on the video, and he listened through earbuds, his sharp CIA-trained senses were fully aware of his surroundings and the people nearby. He wore his standard garb, dark clothes with sunglasses beneath a hoodie. That way he was more likely to blend in and could always keep a watchful eye on people who would have no clue he was looking at them.

He was viewing a silly entertainment tabloid show but he found it unnerving. The two young perky hosts, one male and one female, sat in a loud, brightly colored set, with the words "Entertainment Here and Now" bouncing around the bottom of the screen. The hosts were having a good laugh while footage of the supposed miracles of Richard Abramov played behind them.

"This is what's going viral right here and now across the internet!" the male host said, or rather shouted. Paul grimaced at the young man's unnecessarily loud voice and adjusted the volume of his earbuds.

The image on Paul's device changed to quick cuts of Richard Abramov healing a variety of ailments, along with performing some miscellaneous and seemingly magical acts. A middle-aged woman dropped her crutches and stood. A blind elderly man broke his walking stick over a bony knee to applause as he looked around, obviously able to see the excited onlookers. There was a close shot of Richard holding his hand over wilted flowers in a pot, which then sprang back to life, like time-lapse photography of the buds blooming and stems getting longer as they reached for the sun. Another shot showed a bowl of rotten fruit suddenly swell, becoming full of moist lusciousness. Richard grabbed a pear and bit into it as he passed the bowl around for others to enjoy the delicious fresh produce.

The quality of the shots was inconsistent: some were out of focus, some were shaky, all were amateurish. Still, there was no sense of trickery; it all appeared and felt quite real and astounding.

The two hosts popped back on screen.

"Who is that guy in those clips?!" the female host squealed.

The male host chimed in with his preprepared answer. "Well, we've been told it's billionaire, industrialist, philanthropist, whatever-ist, Richard Abramov. Who is he? No one really knew before. But I guess we will now. And I guess we can add miracle healer to his list now."

They guffawed like two kids who thought they were too cool for school. Paul found them annoying and obnoxious and wished they'd quit editorializing and just get back to the content. He needed to know what was going on with Abramov.

"Those clips are obviously not real," the female host said with an air of faux authority.

"You're right, Amy, the only 'miracle' happening here is the modern trickery of After Effects and Photoshop."

"But there are some claiming he is Jesus come again. Or maybe even God Himself. And that movement is growing."

Finally, some important intel, Paul thought. Though the irony of receiving it through such an idiotic medium was not lost on him.

Jesus returned? Or Isa, as he was referred to by the Islamic father a few days ago?

The timing of this stunt by Abramov with what that father told him made Paul shudder. But he chalked it up as coincidence. Still, the thought made him uneasy.

An incoming call on his device interrupted the program. Paul didn't mind; he'd seen enough. The caller was David Tonklin. Paul accepted it and Tonklin appeared in a window. He looked uncharacteristically stressed. So much so, Paul could practically see him grinding his teeth.

"Where are you, Paul?"

Tonklin always opened with that question. It grated on Paul's nerves. Tonklin spoke to him and others as if they were teens and he was their prying father.

"Downtown," Paul said dryly. And then, almost spontaneously, decided to dip his toe into shark infested waters. "I was just watching a television show. Your boss, Richard Abramov, sure has some strange, extracurricular activities, that's for sure."

The mention of Abramov's name was like a gut-punch to Tonklin. He spasmed and audibly exhaled, which amused Paul, though he dared not show it.

"We don't mention his name, Sheppard, you know that." He only ever referred to Paul by his last name under two conditions: when he was really happy or really angry. It didn't take a genius to figure out how Tonklin was feeling now.

"Why? What difference does it make? He's a business owner who owns a private security firm that has a military contract. That's not really a secret."

"He's a very, very private person," Tonklin said through gritted teeth. He was angry but Paul glimpsed a flicker of something behind the anger that surprised him. *Did I just see a trace of fear?*

"Really?" Paul asked. "He was just in Jerusalem…"

"We are not to mention his name. Period."

The two men just stared at each other over the electronic connection. *How did we get to this place*, Paul thought?

It was about a year ago when the CIA first loaned Paul out to Glass Eye Global Security. He knew Tonklin from their military days and thought it would be fun to reconnect and work together again. Tonklin was vague about who owned the security firm, and the CIA was mum about it too. But in time the name came out. Richard Abramov. Like a little schoolboy with a big secret, Tonklin made Paul swear he would not mention Abramov by name again. Paul agreed with a chuckle, and as soon as he was alone, he did an online search for information about the man. Nothing of significance came up so he put it out of his mind and dismissed Abramov as some eccentric billionaire. One of many in the world.

Then one afternoon many months later, Paul sat in Tonklin's office as they imbibed brandy to celebrate another successful campaign. Paul's mind wandered to the chain of command, something he hadn't done in a long time. *I think I've become too comfortable being just another cog in the machine. But that's the way our superiors want it, right? Just soldier on and don't think about it. Maybe. But it shouldn't be that way. We should think about how our actions affect others. On all sides of a conflict.*

Tonklin could see Paul's attention wasn't with them at the moment, so he decided to pry. "What's on your mind, Paul?"

"Just thinking about the successful airstrike today," Paul commented. "Just like in your old military days, right?"

Tonklin laughed and sipped his drink before he replied. "Not exactly. In the military I had to answer to generals. Here, I have all the freedom I need, and the pay is a lot better."

"Yes, but you still have a boss, right? He gives you the orders, doesn't he?"

Tonklin tensed and went quiet. But Paul wasn't finished.

"Who does the-man-whose-name-we-don't-say take his orders from?"

Tonklin answered him with complete silence. Paul's heart leaped. *Is it possible that Abramov acted independently? That's completely crazy. Even he must follow the direction of a government entity. Right?*

Paul knew he needed to back off. He swirled his drink and sipped it. "Great brandy by the way, Dave. You just must tell me where you get it."

The attempt to diffuse the tension was completely transparent, but Tonklin leapt on it anyway. "It is great stuff. I'll tell you where I get it if you quit that CIA job and come work for me," he said with a sly grin.

Paul was relieved. He'd successfully headed off an uncomfortable situation. "I've told you before, I like my job. I actually have more freedom than I would in the private sector."

"Yeah, well, I think that will be changing soon."

"What do you mean?"

"There have been talks in Congress of changing the charter for firms like mine. The change would include military operations independent of government oversight."

Paul thought for a minute. "Mercenary activity?

"Yes."

"Doesn't Glass Eye do that anyway?" Paul asked, knowing the answer.

"Yeah, but it's all been under the table so far, strictly covert," Tonklin said. "The new charter would put us out in the open."

"So why the change? Why now?"

Tonklin took a deep breath before continuing. "Global terrorist activity has been escalating off the chart in the last few years, particularly since TRIAD appeared on the scene."

"I'm aware of that," Paul replied. He wondered what was so different now.

"A lot of it isn't being reported."

That caught Paul off guard. Being who he was, he should know the level of terrorist activity in the world. But his security clearance only went so high. He was just a cog in the machine, after all. A field agent. Only the top brass sitting in their plush offices at the Pentagon knew everything.

Tonklin elaborated. "By expanding the private sector charter, it's technically kept off the military budget," he said. "Something is brewing and it's big." He sipped his drink and laughed. "It feels like the Apocalypse is coming, my friend, and I stand to make a lot of money off it. You should jump on board while there's still time."

A concerned look crossed Paul's face. He had nothing more to say. "Well, okay then. I'll think about it. Keep me informed."

But they never discussed it again.

"Paul!" Tonklin shouted from the mobile device. "Hey, Sheppard!"

"Oh, sorry. The signal dropped for a second," he said. It was a convincing lie. Part of his job included being a good liar. Paul's mind still lingered a year in the past though.

"Look at this," Tonklin said as he manipulated controls on his end. His image on the tablet shrunk to a smaller box revealing a large crowd, pressing in on itself, gathered before the Great Mosque of Damascus – the Umayyad Mosque.

Paul recognized it immediately. "That's only a few kilometers from here. What's going on? Is this an Islamic holiday or something?"

"No. And those aren't all Muslims. It includes Christians, Jews, Buddhists, Sikhs, Hindus, people from every religion."

"Why?" Paul said, thoroughly confused. He felt a little embarrassed. Being a CIA field agent, he was oftentimes the one gathering and providing intel, not receiving it.

"Some crackpot is holed up inside – a man who many people from around the world believe is Jesus."

Paul's mind immediately went to the Islamic family he met on the day the lousy intel led to the drone strike of a school. *What was it that Muslim man told me? Oh, yeah, he said: It is a sign of the End Times – and the imminent return of Isa. That was the Islamic name for Jesus.*

Paul blinked at the massive crowd several times. "Some crackpot who thinks he's Jesus?" he asked absently. It was phrased as a question but was more of a statement. Then, something dawned on him. "The video I was just watching said the same thing about your boss." He almost said the unspoken name, but he didn't want to antagonize Tonklin anymore than he had already.

"Yeah, whatever," Tonklin said, not having any of it. "I'm sure he has his reasons. But our intel says the guy in the mosque is a terrorist."

"The same intel that said the grade school was a TRIAD stronghold?"

Tonklin shot him a dirty look.

"We need confirmation from boots on the ground. I'll go," Paul said.

"No, you won't. I'm sending you to Jerusalem."

Paul was stunned. "Why?"

"I want you to assist with the cleanup of the Al-Aqsa Mosque and the Dome of the Rock destruction."

"Cleanup duty? I'm an advisor." Paul was offended. He hadn't done any kind of cleanup since the first year on the job. He had felt it was beneath him then and certainly felt even more so now.

Tonklin narrowed his eyes and spoke authoritatively with an air of pompousness. "The CIA has given me authority to use you as I see fit. And that's where I want you. We have a transport waiting."

"I'll drive," Paul said acidly. They both had egos, Paul knew, but Tonklin had mostly driven a desk chair through his career, killing from a distance while he watched it on television. *How dare he tell me – someone who's killed up close – what I'm going to do, and how I'm going to travel.*

"I can be there in four hours," Paul said firmly resolved. Tonklin just glared at him for a moment. Paul knew he was weighing whether he wanted to challenge him on this.

He decided not to. "Fine," Tonklin said. "Go now. I want you on the site first thing in the morning."

"What do you plan to do to the mosque?"

Paul's question stunned Tonklin. He didn't even try to softball it. He could have asked what Tonklin's plans were regarding the mosque, but Paul didn't want to leave room for Tonklin to misinterpret or dodge the question. A direct inquiry requires a direct response.

Except he didn't get one.

"That's on a need-to-know basis, and, right now, you don't need to know."

Tonklin clicked off before Paul could respond. He continued staring at the empty screen for several seconds. It's just as well. Paul wasn't sure he could do anything with the information anyway.

He slipped the tablet into the large pocket of his jacket and walked into the hotel the CIA provided for him. He took the elevator up to his room. He was troubled as his mind returned to the conversation with Tonklin from a year ago, when the man said terrorist activity was increasing around the globe, that it was starting to appear as if the Apocalypse was coming.

Apocalypse? Why would he even say something like that? A religiously fueled word? That wasn't like Tonklin to speak in such terms. In all the time he'd known Tonklin there wasn't a hint of religion in the man. He was a strictly terra firma, nuts-and-bolts kind of man. And that Muslim man in Damascus who spoke of the return of Jesus... or Isa. But I don't believe in any of that stuff.

Paul thought more about Richard Abramov, the man they are not to mention, be it over the phone or in person. The verboten name. The owner of Glass Eye. Paul knew almost nothing about him, except he was a reclusive billionaire that had a finger in everything. At least that was the rumor. One of the elites – a term Paul hated because it was thrown around so much these days. Abramov supposedly was a member of every exclusive club on the planet. As well as every secret society, known and unknown, his name spoken only in whispers with a conspiratorial tone. *Surely, it's all overblown; he's just another rich guy who values his privacy, right?*

But there was *the* incident. Paul hadn't thought about it in so long he'd almost forgotten about it. The yellow journalist who ran that now defunct tabloid. What was the name of it? *The National Watcher*. Yeah, that was it. And the guy who owned it was named Thomas Kincade. A sleazy journalist if ever there was one. Exposing whatever he could about famous people: celebrities, politicians, you name it. Didn't care if it was true. Didn't care whose life he ruined. The lawsuits didn't stop him.

But then one day he announced the story to end all stories. He called it "the greatest story ever told." The same thing Christians said about The New Testament. Kincade said it would be published in the next issue.

But that issue never came out. The offices of *The National Watcher* burned to the ground. With Kincade inside. They said it was suicide. Nothing was salvageable. The fire was ignited by jet fuel and burned so hot as to melt the I-beams that supported the building. It came down like the Twin Towers. That alone got several government agencies involved, including the CIA. Paul was part of the investigation team.

And the rumors floating around were that Thomas Kincade – the owner, publisher, chief editor, and chief journalist of that tabloid rag – was about to release an exposé on none other than Richard Abramov.

But Kincade's death coinciding with the impending Abramov story was just a coincidence, right? But how did he acquire jet fuel? And wasn't it convenient that such a hot fire destroyed everything? No one ever really questioned it. Nor did any journalist ever dig deeper into the life of Richard Abramov. Why? Was it fear? Or did Abramov pull some strings in the background and make interest in him go away? Just who is this man? And how powerful is he?

Then realization slammed into Paul. Hard. *The powers that be, made Kincade go away. And that's exactly what's happening to me. I'm being removed from here, so I don't witness – or try to stop – whatever nefarious action is planned for the Umayyad Mosque.*

For one of the few times in Paul's life, he felt completely helpless.

CHAPTER TWELVE

A beat-up taxi zig-zagged through the ancient streets of Damascus. The passenger in the back seat was unable to speak but wrote a note to the driver, asking him to take him to the Umayyad Mosque nearby. It was one of the largest and oldest mosques in the world, considered to be one of the holiest places in Islam. They arrived midday, and Sadeem quickly paid the driver and hopped out of the taxi.

The magnificent mosque stood before him. Unable to take so much as a moment to appreciate the sight of the pillars and spires, Sadeem rushed up the stone steps and into the building, sweat beading on his brow. Inside the mosque, men and women prayed, and Sadeem moved quietly so as not to disturb them.

A thin man in his forties approached him when he stood for a minute at the back of the prayer room. He shook hands with Sadeem. "I am Jamal. Are you here to see Imam Mahdi?"

Sadeem nodded, glad that the man understood. He followed Jamal down a corridor, and they ducked into a small doorway flanked by lights hung on either side.

*   *   *

Once the equipment cases were placed in the back of the van, Ali slid in behind the wheel. Fatima smoothed the skirt of her black dress as she slipped into the passenger seat and checked her makeup and hair in the visor's mirror. They were looking forward to getting out of Jerusalem for a few days.

"Regardless of what Richard Abramov said to me, what if the mosque and dome were destroyed by TRIAD?" Fatima asked.

"If it was a TRIAD cell, then they need to be hunted down and brought to justice. They do not follow the Muslim ways, nor any of the other faiths associated with them. They are terrorists, plain and simple. I realize they began as an extremist Muslim group, but the Qur'an does not condone what they are doing in the world. I've said many times that Islam is a religion of peace. How we get those evil ones to believe it, I don't know."

Ali started the car and merged with busy traffic. It was bumper to bumper with many drivers honking at each other in irritation. Fatima would be glad to finally leave the congestion and enter the lighter traffic on the countryside roads heading to Damascus.

Ali gathered his thoughts and continued. "Do you remember I mentioned the name Kharijites the day we interviewed the Prime Minister?"

"Yes," Fatima said glancing over at him.

"Many hundreds of years ago, the Kharijites were a sect that broke off from Islam. They have left an indelible and unjustifiable mark that today's terrorists live by, though it is wrong. The Kharijites took the killings of Muslims and non-Muslims as lawful. They rejected the followers who believed in Muhammad's teachings of peace toward all. They were, in fact, the first terrorist group! They challenged the teachings of Muhammad, and turned away from the caliphs, the priests, and the leaders of the faith."

Fatima was confused. "How could that happen? If these… Kharijites…," she said, forming the word slowly, "were there at the beginning, how could they distort the message?"

"Islam is a religion of moderation and balance. But there will always be people who are drawn to extremism."

Fatima nodded as she began to understand what he was saying. "I think I know what you mean. Most religions at one time or another have attracted its own extremists. I know Christianity has had plenty. The Colorado Springs Planned Parenthood killings in 2015. In 2010, nine people belonging to a group called the Hutaree were arrested for planning to kill police officers and civilians using explosives and firearms. The name of the group means 'Christian warriors.' They were preparing for the battle with the Antichrist. Crazy stuff. Most white supremacist groups tend to be Christian, or so they claim."

"That's right. Extremism is not limited to a single religion, as we've seen with TRIAD. The people who committed those terrible acts you mentioned would be considered Kharijites."

He took his gaze off the road for a brief second and looked at Fatima, who listened closely to his words. His strong, passionate emotions on this topic glistened in his eyes. "The modern-day Kharijites brainwash the mullahs, who in turn brainwash the youth. Young boys are being raised by these mullahs to hate the West and believe their roles in life are to kill others and destroy those who don't follow Islam. That is not right. How we get the rest of the world to believe it is another obstacle. With the actions of TRIAD, how can the world understand that is not being a true follower of Islam, or any faith?"

Ali carefully maneuvered through a stoplight before continuing. "As a young boy in Pakistan, my Imam taught us that we are to do good works. That we are to live a righteous life and God will reward us. Not with seventy-two virgins as extremists believe and teach. That is not in the Qur'an, as I often say to anyone who will listen! How they believe those lies, I cannot understand. As the prophet Isa taught, as did the prophet Muhammad, killing others is forbidden. Killing one man is like killing every man, according to the Qur'an. TRIAD has abandoned the book of Muhammad."

"How could it be so misinterpreted?" Fatima asked.

"I remember one verse taught to me long ago," Ali explained. "Chapter 25, Verse 30 says, 'And the Messenger has said, "Oh, my Lord, indeed my people have taken this Qur'an as a book abandoned.' Meaning, that people will one day turn from it, making up their own rules and laws, not keeping the peace among people. And we see it happen, us being in the news business."

Ali turned around a corner, and broke free from the traffic. He and Fatima were relieved to see the open road ahead of them. They knew they would be in Damascus in about five hours. They were leaving behind a city that had just faced the worst terrorist attack in history. And heading to one that was considered one of the most dangerous cities in the world. *Oh, well*, Fatima thought. *Such is the life of a foreign correspondent.*

*   *   *

Sadeem and Jamal spent a few hours meeting with Imam Mahdi behind closed doors. They discussed what Sadeem saw, studied the photo he took, and researched the Qur'an and hadiths for the relevant verses regarding the Dajjal. Additional scholars, teachers, and advisors were called in to consult, and the group concluded the information was important enough for the world to be informed. But it didn't matter that everyone was on the same page. Not if the one who Mahdi was hosting at the mosque – the one who came from the sky – deemed it unimportant.

Sadeem was led to an inner chamber deep within the mosque. As vast and spacious as the mosque was overall, this room was small, dark, and very humble. Sadeem's eyes never really adjusted to it after entering from the much brighter outer chamber. He could see the man kneeling in the prayer position on a prayer rug, but that was really all he could make out. His features were completely hidden. Maybe it was the darkness; maybe it was Sadeem's eyes not adjusting to the lower light;

or maybe Sadeem was just not meant to see this man's features at this time.

"Sadeem?" the man asked warmly.

It was a question, but Sadeem knew the man was just asking out of politeness and convention. This man knew who Sadeem was. In fact, Sadeem instinctively knew, this man knew more about him than he knew about himself.

Yes, Isa, I am Sadeem, he responded via sign language.

The man known as Isa softly laughed. It was a disarming laugh, filled with love, joy, and understanding. "You can speak, Sadeem. You don't need to sign anymore unless you want to."

"Really?" Sadeem asked before he realized he just spoke. His eyes flew wide-open. "You really are who they say you are. Praise Allah!"

Isa laughed again. "There will be time for celebration later. For now, there is much work to be done. You are correct, Sadeem, about the 'man' you believe to be the Dajjal. I knew this vile serpent thousands of years ago. He's been with mankind since the beginning. Summon Mahdi to me, please."

Sadeem nodded and hurried out. With his newfound voice, he told Mahdi and Jamal the contents of his conversation with Isa, and in seconds Mahdi stood before Isa.

"Isa… would you like to deliver the news to the world?" Mahdi humbly asked.

"I am honored, but this is your mosque. You, or whoever you designate, should announce it."

"Thank you," Mahdi said with a respectful nod.

Mahdi conferred with his communications staff who then contacted local and national media. In an unbelievably brief time, a large group of reporters and videographers from the region assembled on the front steps of the mosque like a swarm of bees to a hive. No one from the media had an inkling about what would be discussed. They had only been told it would be significant for the entire world. The media from outside the country paid the necessary licensing fees to pick up the feed as it was considered too dangerous to go into Syria, especially for a news announcement shrouded in secrecy. They were skeptical that the news would be anything of consequence, but since the fees were reasonable, it was better to have it than not.

As the news media impatiently waited in front of the Umayyad Mosque, Paul Sheppard sat behind the wheel of his car idling at a stoplight not too far away. The intersection led to a highway with a sign perched on the shoulder that read: Jerusalem 343 kilometers. It was almost as if the sign was taunting him. Though he would never describe himself as being depressed, at any moment in his life, this was probably the closest Paul was to that feeling.

I'm just a chess piece on the board to be moved wherever the players – the powers that be – want to move me. Or even sacrifice me for the greater good as defined by them. And now one of those players controlling my fate is Richard Abramov. Maybe not directly, but almost certainly and vicariously through Tonklin.

Paul felt he was needed here in Damascus. Maybe he was just fooling himself. If he dug deep into his own thoughts, he might discover he just didn't feel like he should be on the cleanup crew in Jerusalem. Or maybe he was motivated by something else altogether. This supposed return of Isa, perhaps. It startled him to think he thought of this person in terms of his Islamic name. That's what he gets, he assumed, for spending so much time in the Middle East. His reason for wanting to stay could possibly be due to Richard's demonstration as some kind of miracle man. That was so whacky, Paul could hardly wrap his brain around it. Either way, he felt compelled to stay put and investigate what's really occurring here.

But I've been ordered to leave by my superiors, so what am I to do?

The light turned green. But Paul just sat there in indecision. If he pressed the accelerator and drove straight, he would merge onto the highway, and off to Jerusalem he'd go.

What am I going to do?

HONK! It was the car behind him. Paul glanced into the rearview mirror at the angry driver, then made his decision. He accelerated and whipped a U-turn, and then headed back to the city of Damascus.

It was on his way back that he realized why he was doing this. After the drone strike on the grade school which left dozens of people dead, he knew he absolutely must discover whether or not a terrorist had set up shop inside the Great Mosque. If so, maybe he could neutralize him, sparing the lives of thousands of innocent people gathered on the grounds outside the mosque. And if there is no terrorist threat, then he would have to do everything in his power to get Tonklin not to act. Something he tortured himself for not doing before.

I can't waste a second, he thought, as he depressed the accelerator and sped toward the Umayyad Mosque.

Paul inched his car through the massive crowd gathered before the mosque. He found a place to park and got out. He mounted a short stone wall and surveyed the mass of humanity. It had grown significantly from when Paul viewed the footage Tonklin had sent him a little while ago. If he had second thoughts about not heading to Jerusalem, Paul now knew it was a moot point. He was going to be stuck here for a while.

He gazed toward the rooftops, knowing that's where surveillance would be set up by Tonklin or whomever else might be involved in the intelligence gathering. He didn't see anybody peer over the edges but that didn't mean they weren't present.

"Hello, my friend," said an accented male voice from behind him.

Paul whirled about, ready to respond to any threat. But it was just the Islamic man that taught him about Isa. The man stood with his wife and daughter smiling warmly. His daughter had a few bandages on her arms but seemed bright and cheerful. Paul knew kids have a remarkable ability to live in the present and not dwell on the past.

"Hello," Paul said. "Good to see you all again. Glad that you are all well."

The Islamic father beamed. "Words can't describe how we feel."

"Really?" Paul was genuinely interested. With everything that had transpired in the past few days he didn't flippantly dismiss any remarks he heard anymore.

"Yes, we're here to see Isa. The man you would call Jesus."

"You really believe it's him?" Paul asked with the directness and intensity a lawyer would have in directing a question to a witness on the stand.

"Yes! Yes! He is here to battle the Dajjal… the Antichrist. Time is very short."

Paul was alarmed, but he expertly hid it behind a poker face. *Battle? This is not good. A battle in the midst of this crowd could lead to a lot of deaths. Far more than the victims of the school drone strike.*

"Well, I certainly hope it doesn't come to fighting."

The Islamic father spoke with love and patience, like a teacher speaking to a student. "It is written as such. So, it must come to that."

Paul solemnly nodded. No point in arguing a different view. The man believes what he believes. And Paul? Well, he didn't know what to believe.

"I gotta run," Paul said. "But I hope to catch you later. It's been nice seeing you all again."

The father shook his hand. "Good seeing you too, my friend."

Paul nodded and walked off. After he weaved himself through the crowd to put some distance between him and the family, Paul pulled out his phone and made a call.

The operator picked up on the first ring. "CIA, Syrian division."

"ID number 713476. I need to speak to the station chief immediately," Paul said hurriedly.

"Hi, Paul. What can I do for you?" The station chief's voice was pleasant.

"I have strong reason to believe Glass Eye plans to launch an independent attack on a mosque in Damascus within the next few days," Paul said. There was a long pause at the other end. "Did you hear me?"

"Stay out of it, Paul," the station chief said casually.

"What?" He was stunned.

"Just let them do what they need to do. It's not your problem," was the reply before the station chief ended the call.

Paul's jaw dropped. He had never felt so helpless in his entire professional life.

A few hundred feet away, Paul noticed workmen installing large projection screens several stories high across the street. They were positioned at the top of the staircase leading to the entry doors of the mosque. Just as the men put the finishing touches on the installation, the large double doors swung open, and the reporters hopped to attention. The "on" buttons of the cameras were activated and communications vans parked along the street hummed in time for their broadcasts.

A large entourage of men dressed in local garb, along with others in business suits, approached the podium. In his place at the head of the group was Jamal, who waited to speak once the crowd noise died down. He looked around, took a deep breath, then nodded to Sadeem, who stood to his right.

"My name is Jamal. I am the spokesperson for our Imam Mahdi. Thank you all for being here on such short notice. As many of you undoubtably know, Isa, also known as Jesus, has returned to Earth and is now staying in our mosque. With his permission and blessing, we have an important announcement to make to the world." Jamal's voice was steady and strong. "After unmistakable evidence which has presented itself to us, we are very sure of this today." He took a deep breath and raised his voice. "The Dajjal. The Antichrist – who is spoken of in many faiths over many generations – is alive and walking amongst us at this time. We have positively identified him – there is no doubt. According to Islamic teaching, during the End Times, the Dajjal will appear and make his presence known. He will be a man that is missing one eye and performing so-called miracles. We have a photo of such a man taken just a few days ago at a hospital in Jerusalem."

Jamal motioned to an audio-visual technician who then flipped a switch on a control board. One of the massive projection screens above suddenly displayed the still image of Richard Abramov holding his glass eye in the hospital bathroom. It was the photo taken by Sadeem.

Jamal scanned the crowd who stared unblinking at the photo as they hung on his every word. "The Dajjal's name is Richard Abramov!"

Newsrooms around the globe broke into their regularly scheduled programs to air the announcement. At the speaking of Abramov's name, business leaders who knew him looked aghast, thinking about how it would affect business. Heads of state laughed nervously and dismissed the idea as they watched broadcasts with their staff. Celebrities from the western world scoffed, while up-and-coming young athletes were in shock, as his name was connected to many of their sponsorship donations. The philanthropist had been generous across all genres and funds given to ensure the success of future teams. Those worth fortunes wondered if they would lose all the success they had achieved with their connections to Abramov.

In churches, synagogues, and mosques in the Middle East, Europe, Russia, Asian countries, and in the United States, leaders of the faith were shocked at the announcement. Though many didn't believe in the Antichrist anyway, those that did either didn't believe it would happen in their lifetime or had a preconceived notion of how it would transpire, and this announcement from Syria didn't fit what they believed. Nor did they believe Richard Abramov was the Antichrist for no other reason than they had never heard of him. Their preconceptions dictated it must be someone famous or infamous, such as a well-known politician or dictator.

For those faith-based institutions that did believe, each gathered their leaders over the next 24 hours and examined what they knew to be true, based on Scripture and the writings in their holy books.

"How do they know this for sure?" a prominent Christian leader asked a myriad of pastors gathered around the large conference table at a church in Washington, D.C. An open Bible lay in the center of the table, while each man and woman seated referred to one of their own, flipping back and forth between the Old Testament writings and the New Testament scripture that predicts the coming of the Antichrist and the second coming of Jesus. "Just what points to Richard Abramov being the Antichrist? That's the most ridiculous thing I've heard this year!" He pounded his fist on the table for emphasis.

An aide clicked on the television screen, and they viewed a replay of the announcement still being shown around the world. They had to formulate a response, they all believed. For now, they listened without comment to the Muslim speaker.

"To support our conclusions and witness testimony, I will read the following Hadith," Jamal said to the reporters present. His intent was to convey the knowledge Islam had, which came from the prophet Muhammad. "Listen and discern for yourselves, my Christian friends and leaders and those of the Jewish faith. We are all three descended from Abraham, blessed by God all those centuries ago. Inherently, we are connected. This has been written and passed down over the ages. We all struggle with the fight between good and evil, and the Antichrist represents the latter. Isa knew in his time that he would face the Antichrist, therefore we must anticipate confronting this evil soon, based on the evidence!

"The Hadith reads, 'I warn you of him, and there was no prophet but warned his followers of him; but I will tell you something about him which no prophet has told his followers:

Ad-Dajjal is one-eyed whereas Allah is not.' It is the only conclusion we can draw. We have seen that Richard Abramov does indeed have only one eye – we have proof. Many around the world have witnessed videos on the internet of him performing so-called miracles. It is said that the deception created by the Antichrist will lead the world to believe in his power."

Jamal stepped back away from the microphone, allowing the Imam to step forward to speak. "The words I am about to read are from the last sermon of Muhammad, said before he died. We want the world to understand that Islam is indeed a religion of peace. Those who have turned against the righteous path are wrong, and under the influence of the Dajjal. We do not condone killing of others.

"For it is written, '…regard the life and property of every Muslim as a sacred trust. Return the goods entrusted to you to their rightful owners. Hurt no one so that no one may hurt you. Remember that you will indeed meet your Lord, and that He will indeed reckon your deeds…Beware of Satan, for the safety of your religion. He has lost all hope that he will ever be able to lead you astray in big things, so beware of following him in small things…Do treat your women well and be kind to them for they are your partners and committed helpers…All mankind is from Adam and Eve, an Arab has no superiority over a non-Arab nor a non-Arab has any superiority over an Arab; also a white has not superiority over black nor a black has any superiority over white except by piety and good action…'"

Standing at the head of the conference table, the leader asked, "How could the Muslims figure it out? They're not Christian. They don't use the Bible. How?"

A woman at the back of the room, the daughter of a world-renowned pastor who had died the previous year, spoke quietly but with authority. "Apparently, we have more in common with Islam than we thought. We should at least consider, that for such a time as this, as written in the Book of Esther, we all were born. If this is the beginning of the End Times, who are we to question it? And why not now? The world is pretty much a mess, with wars and hate among peoples. We look to Jesus for our strength. Apparently, the Muslims look to him too."

"She is right. We all have a purpose in life. Is this time ours?" one of the other pastors asked. Many nodded, but others were silent. They returned their attention to Jamal on the television broadcast.

"I call all mankind to join us in this final battle. Muslims, Christians, Jews, everyone," Mahdi said in a loud voice. "We need to stand together, united against this evil. The Antichrist is our common enemy! Join us here, in Damascus, for this fight!" He waved his fists to the heavens and offered up a silent prayer before the news team came on adding commentary about the announcement.

"He's right about that, you know," the woman said. "I wish my father were here to witness this."

"What do we do?" The pastors asked among themselves, not sure what to believe.

The leader looked slowly around the table at each person, evaluating their fear and their faith, taking in the scene.

"Do we have the courage to put our faith into action? Our lives have been spent talking about the word of God from the pulpit. Isn't it time we lived the faith? The apostles followed Jesus when he called. Shouldn't we do likewise – be the leaders, the ones to stand against the Antichrist, the Dajjal, as they call him? As dangerous as it's going to be…I'm packing for Damascus. Will anyone go with me? This may be the fight of our lives, and we have to depend on the Lord to lead us," he said.

One by one, they slowly nodded and agreed. The meeting ended with a prayer, and they left the room, each to decide if they had the strength to join the battle.

Across the country in a Jewish synagogue, a group of Orthodox rabbis and teachers all dressed in black pored over the Book of Moses looking for signs. From childhood, they were taught the Messiah will come in a time in the world when he is most needed, when people have turned away from doing good. Perhaps he would come when all is right with the world, as well, but the rabbis knew that was not the case now. The leaders understood there would be much suffering and wars. Scriptures also declare that the lawless one – the Antichrist – or Belial – is said to be a man who will make himself equal to God, having superhuman powers. The indications in the videos bore witness to what Abramov could do.

They studied a photo that a rabbi had displayed on his mobile device. The face of Richard Abramov bore a stone-cold expression. They also noticed that his right eye seemed in its essence very different from his left. Something they would not have noticed had they not watched the broadcast. Was it just their imaginations? They didn't think so. Nonetheless, they were astonished to consider that Richard Abramov might be the Antichrist, and the battle that generations before them had waited for, could begin in these times.

The future was not years away – it was now.

CHAPTER THIRTEEN

Fatima and Ali had driven in silence along a long, straight, narrow road toward Damascus for more than an hour. Fatima enjoyed the view of the passing landscape beneath a serene blue sky with a smattering of puffy, white clouds. Looking at it, one would never know the chaos and tension brewing in the world right at this moment. After a while she dozed off.

An hour later, Fatima was wide awake and felt rested. She fished her tablet out of her purse, found a cell signal, and tuned into the news.

"Let's see what's happening in the world now," she mused as she logged onto the *News World* website.

Ali chuckled. It was one of those laughs that said he didn't think anything of significance could have happened in the last couple hours.

Boy, was he wrong. They watched a replay of Mahdi's press conference, on the top landing in front of the Umayyad

Mosque's grand entry doors, announcing Richard Abramov as the Antichrist.

Fatima followed that with a search through other news links. The name of Richard Abramov appeared in several articles, along with many photos in different settings. Abramov at a hospital. Abramov at a fundraising gala. Abramov in Africa standing among school children.

"He's everywhere," Fatima observed as she scanned the photos. "Just a few days ago I couldn't find a single photo of him on the internet, and now there are dozens."

"I guess the dam has broken," Ali said.

She moved through the images. "They can't all be from the last few years, but, oddly, he looks exactly the same age in all of them."

Ali gave her a proud smile. "Well, apparently you had the scoop of the millennium. Actually, the greatest scoop in history, and you didn't tell the world."

"Because it was crazy."

"Doesn't sound so crazy now, does it?"

"No."

Fatima clicked through a few more links with stories about Richard Abramov. "If it wasn't for what I'd experienced at Abramov's palace I'd think…," she couldn't finish the thought, couldn't go down that rabbit hole. She feared she might never find her way back out.

"I know, Fatima, I know," Ali said softly. "But I've examined in my head the teachings of my faith. I… really think… the evidence is pointing to this reality. I am frightened of what this will mean for the world. Yet think of this: it also means it is time for the second coming of Isa. In our lifetime! The man you might have the chance to interview in Damascus is sounding more and more like the real deal."

Fatima was speechless. She looked at Ali with alarm. Shaking her head, she remembered what her mother had taught her, though she hadn't thought about it for years. She was raised to believe that Isa, born of Maryam, was a prophet of Allah, who would be taken up to heaven, but return one day as the Messiah. But he was only someone "out there" in the atmosphere, in the heavens, not here on Earth. Even with everything she'd experienced, everything that was happening in the world at this moment... could it mean that Isa had returned? Although they were making this trip to Damascus to interview this man, she just now realized that deep in her heart and soul, she wasn't sure she was ready to go there yet.

She felt it was better to refocus on Richard Abramov. As absurd as it sounded to her, she thought it was easier to wrap her head around the idea of the Antichrist walking amongst them, than the concept of the returning Messiah.

"What is the Antichrist supposed to do to the world?" she asked. "Will we see violence and death?"

"Yes, Fatima, Islam teaches about the Masih ad-Dajjal, the false messiah, and his followers," he explained. "He is an anti-messianic figure, comparable to the Antichrist in Christian eschatology and to Armilus in Jewish eschatology. Islam also teaches that the Dajjal has influenced and corrupted the true Islamic faith, causing chaos and division in the world. Take

TRIAD, for example. That is a result of the Dajjal. They do not practice love, peace, and mercy. They are killers! That does not uphold the true heart of our faith. If the appearance of the Dajjal in the form of Richard Abramov is true, then we'd better be prepared for truly meeting Isa when we get to Damascus. If he indeed is the Messiah as predicted in Islam, as I'm beginning to be convinced, then we are in the midst of the Second Coming! I'm a solid believer in Islam, but what is happening right now is so fantastical that it even tests my faith."

Fatima was overwhelmed with how many more stories there were about Abramov than the man who may or may not be Isa. She set her tablet in the passenger seat footwell and leaned back in her seat. "Why is it so easy to believe that the Antichrist could be here, but not Isa?"

Ali shrugged, staring straight ahead as he gripped the steering wheel. "I don't know. Probably because there have been so many movies made about the Antichrist it's easier for one to wrap their mind around it."

"Good point."

Ali solemnly nodded and kept his eyes on the road. "You know, Fatima, the night we watched the video after we got back from the palace, and saw it conflicted with your story, I worried about your mental health." He took a deep breath. "But not anymore. With Abramov in the news just a day later, performing 'miracles', I now completely believe you. And I believe Abramov is the Dajjal."

"Yeah… so do I." Then she added softly, "I think, I always knew."

Ali was stunned. "Really?" he asked as he glanced over at her.

"Yeah," she said as she stared straight ahead, but not really looking at the road. It was as if she was looking back in time, into her own past.

She took a deep breath. "Remember when I said I attended a university in Saudi Arabia?"

"Yes, of course."

"Well, my uncle, the Imam, took me on a pilgrimage to Mecca, for Hajj. The whole family went, so I was required to go."

Ali gaped at her, then grinned. "I know it's wrong, Fatima, but I am so jealous. I've never been to Mecca but would love to go."

Fatima smiled at him. "Life is filled with little ironies, Ali. I went begrudgingly because I didn't have a choice. But while there, something strange happened."

Ali knew he had to keep his eyes on the road, but he couldn't help but steal glances at her as he hung on her every word.

She gathered her thoughts and went on. "As you know, during the Hajj, we must circle the Kaaba."

"Yes, yes," he said impatiently. "We must walk around it seven times, counterclockwise, to make sure it remains on our left side. Please go on."

She smiled at him, amused by his eagerness. But the thought of what happened in Mecca unnerved her. She took a deep breath and continued. "I joined the unbelievably massive crowd and started walking around the Kaaba, and before I knew it, I felt deep joy and contentment, feelings I never recall feeling before in any aspect of my Islamic faith."

"You felt the presence of Allah."

"I guess so," she said with a shrug. "Then I looked at the Kaaba and marveled at the awesomeness of this massive, cube-shaped structure. I tilted my neck further and further until I was looking into the sky… and…"

Fatima shook her head and seemed to pale a little.

"What? What?" Ali exclaimed. He was beside himself, wanting to know what she experienced.

"In the sky… I saw… eyes… enormous eyes… two of them… spaced apart like they would be on a human face. One eye appeared normal. But the other was horrifying… blood red and rimmed with fire. And they were filled with hatred. For us. For humanity. I saw those same eyes again when I was at Abramov's mansion. Those were his eyes."

Ali blinked several times at the thought of what Fatima saw that day. "Did anyone else see those eyes in the sky?"

"I don't think so. I blinked and they were gone. But the feeling of dread lingered for several seconds. I looked around at the huge crowd and everything seemed normal. Soon the blissful feeling returned, and I continued my trek around the Kaaba. I chalked the experience up to the heat of the sun. Just a touch of dehydration. Put it out of my mind. Until I stood facing Richard Abramov in his mansion. Then those memories came flooding back. So yes, I believe that Richard Abramov is the Dajjal." Even with her experience at Mecca, Fatima could hardly believe she admitted that, considering how far she had backslid in her faith over the last dozen or so years.

She looked out the window and prayed a silent prayer – to whom, she didn't know. *Allah, if you're out there, if you can hear me after all these years, please stop this madness.*

*   *   *

They drove in silence for some time, Fatima dozing, and Ali lost in his own thoughts. He journeyed mentally into his past, to when he was a small boy and first introduced to Islam and the Qur'an. He pondered the lessons he'd been taught about Muhammad and his teachings. He thought back to Muhammad's life and wished he could have been a witness to those astounding events.

*   *   *

Around 610 CE, Muhammad, an extremely spiritual and religious man, who spent months in prayer and contemplation in a secluded cave near the town of Mecca, received divine messages from the Archangel Gabriel. He heard only the angel's voice. Through Gabriel, Allah spoke words of wisdom. The words were recited by Muhammad, then later by his disciples, then recorded as text, which became the Holy Qur'an.

Islam literally means "submission." The faith was founded on the teachings of the Prophet Muhammad, as spoken to him by Gabriel, and as written down in the Qur'an. Traditional Muslims believe that Allah is the one true God with no partner or equal.

Many people were impressed by the verses of the Qur'an and freely converted to Islam. But the growing popularity of Islam jeopardized Muhammad's and his followers' lives, so the entire community moved from Mecca to Medina circa 622 CE.

This was a pivotal event in the history of Islam and came to be known as Hijarh. The first day of the migration marks the beginning of the Muslim calendar. Later, Muhammad converted Mecca as well, along with other parts of Arabia.

The followers of Islam are traditionally divided into two main branches, the Sunni and Shia. Although each group follows the same religion, they interpret certain events and teachings in Islam differently.

Muhammad's message was essentially the existence of one God who was all powerful but merciful. He freely acknowledged that other prophets – particularly Abraham, Moses, and Isa – preached the same truth in the past.

In fact, Muslims were instructed in the Qur'an to be tolerant of the two older and closely related religions, Judaism and Christianity, which share with Islam the essential characteristics of monotheism and a sacred book. They are all linked in the phrase "People of the Book." Jews and Christians have, for the most part through history, fared better under Islam than Jews or Muslims have in Christian countries.

During the 7th through the 11th centuries, Islam had expanded from the Indus in the east, and across North Africa to southern France, to the Iberian Peninsula in the west. Muslims did not require total submission by Jews and Christians to Islam.

Nonetheless, military campaigns led by Christians, primarily against Muslims, were conducted from 1095 to 1291 CE. These were called The Crusades. The goal was to establish control of Jerusalem – called the "City of God" by Christians – the city where Isa had taught. Muslims were also determined to keep the city, where the Islamic prophet, Muhammad had taught. This led to some of the most brutal warfare in human history, costing millions of lives.

After two centuries and many crusades to the Holy Land, the will of the Europeans began to wane. This was due to the lack of desire the Christians had for fighting in the Holy Land and the back-and-forth nature of the conflicts with the Muslims. Throughout the Crusades, Jerusalem changed hands multiple times between the Christians and the Muslims.

Ultimately, the Ninth Crusade was the final one, and the Christians lost control over the Holy Land to the Muslims.

Islam continued its expansion, and between 1453 and 1526 CE Muslims founded three major states: The Ottoman Empire in the Mediterranean, the Safavid Empire in Iran, and the Mughal Empire in South Asia. Muslims won converts everywhere, and many people practiced Islam without abandoning the practices of their previous faith. After the establishment of the three states, some of the greatest Islamic artistic achievements were made, which impressed even the Europeans. It was in this period the Muslims formed the cultural patterns that they have brought into the present age, and faithfulness to Islam grew to approximately its current distribution.

Ali was pleased that he could remember all this history that he had been taught from early childhood into his teen years. He caught a quick glance of the smile on his face in the car's rearview mirror, then turned his gaze back to the road ahead.

CHAPTER FOURTEEN

Paul mingled with the masses to assess the situation. Crowds of people walked toward the mosque, answering the call to arms issued by Imam Mahdi against the Antichrist. They came from all directions and were a mix of all ages and forms of dress – Middle Eastern and Western, dresses, pants, and jeans. Some were young, while others were old. Some came in wheelchairs and others on bicycles. Paul noticed the people seemed to be of different faiths, based on their clothing. The rabbis wore long, dark robes. The Christian pastors carried Bibles. The Muslim women were dressed in hijabs. A few wearing burkas were in the crowd, but most of the women wore brightly colored dresses. The people were loud and boisterous, full of joy and energy.

As Paul made his way through the crowd, he overheard something that stopped him dead in his tracks. In broken English, a man clearly said, "Isa returned several nights ago. From the sky. I saw him myself."

Paul quickly scanned the crowd and found the man. He was an older fellow, short and plump. He waved his hands in excitement before a small crowd, gesturing like someone in the midst of a medical emergency. But it was elation that drove him.

"It was the most transcendent thing I've ever witnessed!"

"And it was Isa?" asked an onlooker.

Paul could tell by the questioner's demeanor that he and his group were not part of the crowd drawn here by the Imam's call. They were here to gawk and make fun of the participants.

"Yes! Without a doubt!" the short, portly man stated with conviction.

"Did he say he was Isa?"

"No."

"Then how can you be certain?"

"Because I knew when I looked into his eyes." The man's smile glowed with enthusiasm.

Paul listened with fascination. The man's belief in what he experienced was so deep and intense, Paul was half-convinced.

*   *   *

There were at least a thousand people in the mosque, yet hardly a sound; it was that quiet. Everyone was in a massive circle facing the center as though watching a chess match and daring not to breathe for fear of disturbing the players. Near the center stood Imam Mahdi, his assistant Jamal, and Sadeem, the man who started the ripple throughout the world by bringing the dreadful news of the Dajjal.

In the center was another man. Silent. Pondering. Confident. He paced back and forth, his rubber-soled shoes making the only sound in the place. He was the center of everyone's attention. Mahdi nervously fidgeted with his light tan robe. Normally, he never felt apprehensive in his own mosque; never out of sorts; always in control. But these weren't normal times. These "times" went by many names. The End Times. The End of Days. The Last Days. He took a deep breath and stepped forward.

"Isa," he said softly.

The pacing man stopped and faced him. Though he was dressed in modern clothing and appeared as normal as any man in the room, everyone knew he was a man from another time, another place. A place that was beyond comprehension. He smiled warmly at Mahdi. The smile was magical and moved through the room like an invisible wave, putting everyone at ease.

"Yes, Mahdi?" he asked.

"Could you lead the morning prayer?"

"I am honored. But this is your mosque, and you are the Imam of the community. You should lead the prayer."

Mahdi nodded. "As you wish."

*   *   *

Paul Sheppard felt helpless. There was no chance of an evacuation. He was just one man and there were thousands of people here, and the crowd continued to grow by the minute.

He knew it would take hundreds, if not thousands, of trained personnel to organize such an event. Not to mention the dozens upon dozens of buses to move people to a safer area.

He decided on a more direct, overt approach. Speaking to the Islamic family, and overhearing the man who believed Isa had returned, gave Paul the idea for what he needed to do. Maybe the mosque's Imam and Isa himself can do the work for him by telling these people to leave. But he would have to convince them first.

Paul mounted the front stairs, two at a time, until he reached the massive wooden doors of the Umayyad Mosque. He tried the doors. They were locked, of course. He expected as much. But he wasn't giving up that easily. He commenced pounding, feeling he'd give it a go until he risked injuring himself. Fortunately, he didn't have to keep it up too long before he heard keys jingling in the lock. They sounded like large, old-fashioned keys, possibly as old as the mosque itself.

Paul stepped back as the door cracked open. An Islamic cleric peered out. He was an ancient man with leathery skin and eyes full of wisdom.

"May I help you?"

"I need to speak to whoever's in charge. You are in danger," Paul said firmly with an air of authority about him.

"We are always in danger," the cleric responded, unmoved by Paul's insistence.

"There's going to be an attack."

"By whom?"

"By…," the words caught in Paul's throat. His shame came on so suddenly, it surprised him. He took a breath and started again. "By my people."

The cleric's eyes widened. "Americans?"

"It's more complicated than that, but that's part of the answer."

"Why should we believe you?"

"Because I'm telling the truth," Paul said as sincerely as possible. This was hard for him, because, being in the CIA, he was in the business of deception and misinformation. The U.S. government had spent much money and time training him for just such things.

"I'll let the appropriate people know," the cleric said with a sense of finality as he closed and locked the door.

He did it so swiftly, he caught Paul off-guard. "Wait! Wait!" he said as he pounded again on the door. But there was no answer.

Disheartened, Paul turned and looked over the crowd. He had a magnificent view from the vantage point of the landing at the top of the steps.

Paul was a man of action and would never choose to stand around doing nothing, no matter how dire the situation seemed. So, he snapped a few photos of the crowd on his cell phone camera just in case he needed them later. As a CIA agent, carrying a fancier, digital camera would be cumbersome, so he had always opted for using the camera built into his phone. He sent them to his cloud storage and pondered what to do next. *I have to try to get Tonklin to understand.*

As if on cue, his phone rang. It was Tonklin. "Hey, chief, Paul here." He tried to keep his voice steady.

"Where are you?" Tonklin's voice was angry.

"In my car outside the hotel in Jerusalem," he lied.

"No, Paul, you're not. I have on-the-ground reports that say you drove to Damascus. Now I want to know why!" Tonklin was mad and Paul had to think fast.

He hesitated. "Look, Tonklin, I wanted to be on the ground in case I could be of any help if you went through with attacking this mosque. I'm still hopeful you and your boss will call off this horrific plan."

"We're not calling it off, Paul! We take orders from Abramov now and we don't question them. You must know that. You've made a big mistake, Sheppard. You are out as my contractor. I am cutting off all the communication and special passes you hold. They are worthless. You're on your own, my man. Any return ticket to the States in your name has been canceled. Good luck, buddy. You're on the wrong side!" The call clicked off and Paul stood stunned.

He took a few deep breaths to calm himself. His hands shook, and his heart pounded in his chest. *I should have seen it coming. Glass Eye and its actions have long been investigated by the CIA, yet everyone turns their backs on obvious evidence. Abramov's been behind it all along. Guess I'll be looking for a new job – even the CIA can't be trusted anymore.*

With quiet desperation, he scanned the thousands of people that filled the streets for blocks. *These people are going to need a miracle.*

Just then, Paul spotted a white van entering the crowd from a side street and painstakingly inch its way as close to the mosque as possible before it became too compressed and bottlenecked within the vast mass of humanity. The driver and passenger doors opened and out stepped a man and woman. They appeared to be of Middle Eastern descent, Paul assessed, but it was hard to tell. They could really be from anywhere. Olive skin and jet-black hair doesn't always equate with people from the Middle East. They certainly didn't dress as though from here. In fact, they were cosmopolitan in dress and demeanor.

The man pulled professional camera gear from the back of the van. With a video camera propped on his shoulder, the couple made their way up the lengthy flight of stairs leading to the mosque.

As they got closer, Paul could truly see how beautiful the woman was. They continued past him as if he weren't even there.

"You guys are the media, right?" Paul asked.

They stopped and looked back at him with a touch of suspicion mixed with curiosity. The woman looked at her companion's video camera, then smirked at Paul.

"Obviously," the woman said, condescendingly.

"I can use your help," Paul said before they turned away from him.

"How so?" she asked, over her shoulder.

"I believe this place is going to be attacked soon. Possibly an airstrike."

"Sure, it is," she said, obviously not believing him. "Besides, how could we help?"

"By getting the word out. Putting it on the air. Telling the people to evacuate."

"How would you even know this?" Ali chimed in as he shifted the weight of his camera slightly on his shoulder.

"Because I'm with the CIA."

"You'd have to prove that before we'd listen to anything you say."

"Sure."

Paul pulled his wallet from his pocket. He opened it up and showed him his CIA ID. The man and woman gawked in shock at it, which surprised Paul.

"What's the big deal? It's just my ID."

But that's not what had their attention. Next to his CIA identification was another one that stated: GLASS EYE GLOBAL SECURITY – PAUL SHEPPARD.

A knowing smile curled on the lips of the woman as she looked Paul in the eyes. Paul recognized that expression. It was one a person might have when hitting the jackpot at a casino, or when having a winning poker hand.

She thrust her hand out at him to shake.

"Hi, Paul. I'm Fatima. And this is Ali. We're with *News World*."

Before Paul could respond, the whine of electronic feedback drew everyone's attention to the front of the mosque. Imam Mahdi, Jamal, and others crowded near the podium set up at the top of the impressive stone and marble staircase. Mahdi positioned himself directly in front of the podium; his image filled the several story-tall, video projection screens.

A hush passed through the massive crowd that filled the streets. Mahdi had everyone's undivided attention.

"What's going on?" Fatima asked him, keeping her eyes on Mahdi.

"I have no idea," Paul answered.

"May I have your attention, please," Mahdi said. Though he spoke softly, his voice boomed from the huge, concert-sized speakers and echoed for blocks off the surrounding buildings.

"Isa has asked me to give the morning prayer."

Paul threw Fatima and Ali a look. "Apparently there is a person in the mosque that claims to be Isa, or Jesus."

Fatima and Ali exchanged knowing glances.

*   *   *

From his mansion in Jerusalem, the Dajjal stood and looked out over the countryside through his control room's large, one-way windows. Guards provided by Glass Eye Global Security were outside the room's steel-reinforced doors. Though he had had many guests over to his mansion these past decades – centuries, actually – very, very few were ever privileged to see this chamber. It had been frequently remodeled and updated over the years as technology advanced. Rules of engagement prevented him from cheating by using technological advances not indigenous to the time-period. But he always kept it cutting-edge with what was available at the time. Today was no different.

Inside were gathered 20 men dressed in hooded, black tunics, each holding an assault rifle. The Dajjal turned to them, his one good eye blood-red and angry, showing the depths of a world dark and far away, fire shooting from within. The glass eye was not in its socket, but stored in a velvet-lined box, tucked in his jacket pocket. He seethed, his chest expanding as spit flew from his mouth, a cruel grin on his face. His face was ancient with deep lines of the centuries, and at the same time, his appearance would intermittently change to be youthful and of the modern day.

"Ah, my army of deceivers, lieutenants in my latest terrorist organization called TRIAD," he said. "The mosque in Damascus has announced my identity to the world. Not important, as most will ignore the message. And soon the mosque will be no more and the one that has returned will be dead amongst the ruins. We now have control of the government in the United States after a successful infiltration into their respective computer systems. Next, we move to take control of those in Syria and Israel, as we start to move into other countries. My minions should have that feat accomplished within the hour. The booty will soon be divided, and most of the world left penniless, except for those who follow my commands. Many business leaders, politicians, and heads of state have been loyal to me, and they will now be repaid. You too will be given your share. Now go and create more chaos wherever you can. Keep the world in fear and distracted from what is really going on. Make me proud."

The men dutifully turned and filed out of the room through a secret passageway that took them beneath the mansion grounds to the airstrip.

The Dajjal grinned to himself. He controlled many of the world's governments, and so many private companies it would be impossible to keep track of if he were a normal human. And he also controlled Glass Eye Global Security and TRIAD, two organizations on opposite ends of the spectrum, forever locked in combat. It was like playing both sides of the chess board. No matter the outcome, he's the winner. The thought warmed the dark pit in his chest that passed for a heart.

*   *   *

After the morning prayer ended, Paul, Fatima, and Ali stepped off to the side of the Great Mosque. Paul filled them in, on who he was and what he knew. He made sure to steer clear of anything that would violate his confidentiality agreement with the U.S. government or Glass Eye Global Security, but he did tell them that his boss from that organization, Tonklin, gave him the boot.

Ali listened like a rapt child hearing a marvelous story told by a parent. Fatima, although listening intently, kept a veil of healthy skepticism over herself. Yes, Paul worked for the CIA and Glass Eye, but maybe he was a disinformation agent. Or a liar. Or just plain crazy. Nonetheless, she heard him out. Paul explained that someone – likely Abramov – had ordered a strike on the mosque. Glass Eye was involved and allowing it to happen.

"Do you know when they plan to attack?" Fatima asked.

Paul solemnly shook his head, then informed them he was fired as Glass Eye's government advisor, so he's now cut off from their intel. "And I have no idea where I stand with the CIA right now," he added.

"I'm sorry," Fatima said indifferently. She didn't know him well enough to feel bad for him. Not yet anyway.

Ali shook his head. "Yeah, man. Sorry to hear that. But look, you made the right choice to try to warn the Imam, at least that's what I think."

"We have to warn them. We need to get everyone out of the building," Paul said. "All they need is to have the place full of those who have answered the Imam's call when the attack comes. There's been enough bloodshed and destruction in the past few days."

They moved back to the front of the mosque, working their way through the heavy crowd. They moved quickly, Fatima and Ali politely excusing themselves as they gently squeezed their way past people. But not Paul. He was an impatient man on a mission.

"This may sound strange at this point, guys, but I don't have a head cover," Fatima said. "Will they let me in?"

Paul laughed. "You're joking, right? There are so many people here, I'm sure no one will notice. Trust me. If it's a problem, you can use my handkerchief."

They reached the front doors of the mosque. Paul faced Fatima and Ali. "The last time I tried to get in, I failed."

"Well, part of being a journalist is getting into places others can't," Fatima said. "So, let me give it a try."

She stepped up and pounded on the door.

"Are you sure Glass Eye Global Security will follow through on what Abramov wants?" she asked Paul.

"Yes," he said directly and without hesitation.

A moment later, the same Islamic cleric that rejected Paul, cracked the door open.

"May I help you?" he asked Fatima.

"I'm with the media and would like to talk to Isa," she said with tempered confidence. She learned a long time ago that being too forceful easily turned people against helping.

The Islamic cleric was not impressed. "He is granting no interviews," he said with a quick eye roll.

"We would like to help him get his message out," she said undaunted.

"He needs no help."

Before Fatima could respond, Ali tapped her on the shoulder. She threw him a quizzical look as he stepped up to the door.

"Oh, most holy teacher," he began, with his arms spread respectfully. "I have done research on this most glorious mosque, and I see the Imam is named Mahdi. I have studied and learned that Imam Mahdi, meaning 'the Rightly Guided One', is a figure in Islamic eschatology who will appear during the End Times to rid the world of evil and injustice. Muslim tradition states he will appear alongside Isa and establish the Divine Kingdom of Allah."

The cleric was duly impressed, so Ali went on.

"We are here on urgent business, and it is imperative, that we speak now to the Imam."

Ali drew the cleric's attention to Paul. "This man is from the United States and has learned of an impending attack being planned against this, our Great Mosque. Please, we need to ask the Imam to help clear out the people, or they will lose their lives."

The elderly cleric stood, a look of shock on his face, not sure he believed what Ali had told him. "I don't know…"

Paul spoke next, plainly and to the point. "He speaks the truth. I work for the CIA and today, I have learned that Mr. Richard Abramov – the alleged Antichrist – is behind the plan to destroy this mosque and kill everyone here."

The cleric pulled the door open all the way and motioned for the three to enter. He quickly closed and locked it, then he motioned them to follow him down a lengthy, ornate corridor.

"If you say the man planning the attack is Richard Abramov, that is good enough for me. We do not want to assist him in any of his evil plans to hurt humanity. He has done enough damage, turning the people against their faith, leading others to kill in the name of Allah. Yes, this way. The Imam is in here." He opened the door to a large room decorated in ancient stylings, with luxurious curtains that were stitched in gold and silver threads. He greeted the Imam as he quickly told him the guests came with an urgent message before he allowed the other three to enter.

The Imam stood and dismissed his aide. "What is this you have to tell me? And how can I help?" He came closer to the three, so he could hear all they had to say.

Paul spoke for the group. He shook the Imam's hand and introduced himself and the others. With the formalities out of the way, he got to the point and explained the situation.

The Imam was quiet, contemplating what Paul had told him. He walked to the window and gazed upon the masses. "I have called them to me, and they have responded. They are full of joy at wanting to fight the Dajjal. The people want to work together, and this does not happen every day. Usually there is division and anger. But not today. These people who have come from all parts of the world and are of different faiths and cultures. Yet they are not fighting, but rather, they are cooperating instead. Everyone who has come, knows the risks."

"Even those who came with families?" Paul asked.

"Especially those with families."

It was Fatima who spoke next. "Is it true that Isa has returned?"

Paul and Ali stared at her, unblinking. The room fell so quiet Fatima thought she could hear her own heartbeat. Ali was curious as to the answer to this question. Paul was concerned that such a question could derail everything he was trying to do. The Imam slowly turned and faced them. He looked from one to the other, taking his time, weighing his words.

"Yes," he finally said.

Paul was fascinated by the answer. And a little perplexed. He furrowed his brow, and he rolled the concept around in his mind. It's one thing for a man in the crowd outside to claim Isa had returned, but it's quite another to hear it from one of the most renowned spiritual leaders of one of the biggest faiths on the planet.

"How can you be sure that he is the real deal?" Fatima asked.

"Because once in his presence, you just know."

"How did he arrive?" Paul asked.

Ali cringed. It seemed to him that Fatima and Paul were ganging up on Mahdi.

Mahdi silently pointed upward.

"From the sky?" Paul prodded.

"Yes. Descended from the vastness above us," Mahdi said. He anticipated the next question, so he answered it. "Witnessed by the gathered thousands." To punctuate his point, he motioned to the window that he'd been looking out of moments ago.

Fatima chimed in with a question. "May I speak to him?"

All eyes were on Mahdi as he considered her request. But before he could answer, the door to an inner chamber opened, and Jamal stepped out. "Isa will see Fatima now," he said. Paul, Fatima, and Ali were taken aback, but only briefly. If it was a trick, it was a simple one. Something that could easily be done with hidden microphones in the room. Nothing impressive at all.

Mahdi nodded and motioned Fatima toward the inner door. Paul and Ali started to follow.

"Just Fatima," Jamal said.

Paul threw Fatima a concerned look. He was a CIA agent, after all, and they were in a very dangerous, foreign country. No telling what could lie within the darkened room. She could tell by his disposition that he was skeptical and worried.

"It's okay."

"You sure?"

She grinned. "You might be a CIA field agent, but I'm a television journalist. I've been in questionable situations before. I don't think this is one of those times. Got a good feeling about it."

Her reassurance didn't ease his tension, but there was nothing he could do. He gave a stone-faced nod.

Jamal stepped aside, and Fatima walked past him, disappearing into the dark room. He closed the door and moved over, alongside Mahdi. The four men remained quiet. And waited.

Fatima stood just inside the room waiting for her eyes to adjust to the darkness. She slowly became aware that candles were the only light source. At the far end of the room a man kneeled in prayer, his back to her. After a moment, he stood and faced her. There was nothing remarkable about him. At least in appearance. He wore an untucked light-yellow, long-sleeved shirt, neutral-colored slacks, and soft-soled shoes.

He sported a well-groomed, close-cropped beard, and his hair was a little long, but not excessively so. Nothing remarkable about him at all.

He stepped toward her and then she saw his eyes. There was a distinct twinkle in them, a glow that seemed to reach into eternity, and shined a light into the very depths of her soul. *This is just the flickering candlelight, right?*

"I'm Isa. Pleased to meet you."

The greeting was so normal and casual it pulled her out of her daze. Nonetheless, the experience was dreamlike and otherworldly. In many respects it was like when she met Richard Abramov. But at the same time, it was the opposite of that experience. With Abramov, there was a deep feeling of unease. Here, she felt safe and content. And fulfilled. Still... she had to know.

"*The* Isa? The Qur'an Isa?" She asked.

"Yes," he said with a grin.

Even with the comfortable feeling she had in being near him, it was just too much to blindly believe.

"I'm sorry, I don't mean to be rude, but... I just never... I don't believe really... maybe at one time... but even if I did now, you sound so...," she shook her head, unable to finish her thought.

He finished it for her. "I sound too normal? Regular? Like everyone else?"

"Something like that."

He shrugged. "I sounded 'normal' to the people I walked amongst two thousand years ago as well," he said with a warm smile. "Why should now be any different?"

"If that is true, that you were here, alive two thousand years ago – and I'm not saying whether it is or not – people struggled with belief even then, back when it was easier to believe such things, because the world was…" she paused as she searched for the right word.

"Simpler?" he asked, amused. "Less sophisticated?"

"I suppose. I don't mean to offend."

"You're not. But just because life was different then, less technological, doesn't mean people were simpler. Not everyone anyway. People gave concepts and ideas a great deal of thought. There was still a lot of disbelief then, regarding who I was. And am."

"Then shouldn't you do things differently now? To make it easier to believe?" Fatima asked.

"You mean appear in a major way so the world can see me? Perform miracles that can't possibly be tricks, or hoaxes, or movie special effects, right?"

"Exactly."

"Because faith isn't faith if it's certainty. People must come to Allah with faith. Not just to Allah, but to all his messengers."

"Are you who people say you are?"

Gentle laughter bubbled up in him. "People say I'm a lot of things."

"You know what I mean."

"Yes," he said with a warm smile. "But I'm waiting for you to say it."

She looked him firmly in the eyes for several seconds. "Are you the Messiah?" she finally asked.

His eyes almost seemed to twinkle with joy and amusement. "What do you think?"

"I don't believe in the Messiah."

"Why would you ask me if I'm something that you don't believe in?"

That stumped her. She put on her journalist's thinking cap and regrouped. "Well, I'm open to being convinced otherwise. But it would require proof."

"What kind of proof are you looking for?"

"You're just stalling," she said with a chuckle, not trying to be confrontational or offensive. "How about a miracle?"

"Miracles don't come on demand. I'm not a stage magician. They have a time and place at Allah's choosing."

She pondered his response and then pressed on, looking him straight in the eyes. Those incredible eyes. "Why are you here?"

"Because it's time for me to be here."

Fear gripped her. "What's going to happen?" The question was so soft, it was barely a whisper.

For the first time since she entered the room, Isa's smile faded. Not in an angry way, or sad way, but in a more serious manner.

"What needs to happen," he said, and a cold chill ran down her spine.

*   *   *

After her meeting with Isa, Fatima grappled with conflicting emotions. His presence brought a newfound love and contentment, yet the unsettling idea of prophetic End Times lingered.

As thoughts of what might be coming raced through her mind, she found solace by a mosque window overlooking the vast crowd.

Then, the Azaan echoed – the Muslim call to prayer – from a nearby minaret that was atop a soaring, pencil-thin tower. The soothing cadence tugged at her, awakening something long dormant. Unsure whether it was real or imagined, she decided it didn't matter; she felt compelled to act.

In a private restroom, Fatima performed her ablution, cleansing her face, arms, head, and feet with flawless, familiar motions she gained from her teenage years of doing this often. It was basically a Wudu ritual, but she wasn't sure she should think of the cleansing in that way since she hadn't performed the ritual in so long.

Afterwards, she joined those gathered for prayer in the mosque, discreetly using the edge of a large prayer carpet. She could feel the power of her prayer coursing through her. It was a sensation so long forgotten that it felt refreshingly new.

But Fatima knew she still had a way to go before her faith was completely restored.

CHAPTER FIFTEEN

From his secure study in his home in London, the Dajjal viewed the online news reports from the various television stations around the world. His plan was working, as those members of his group obeyed his orders to continue to air stories about him and the "miracles" he had performed in previous weeks. He wanted the world to know who he was and what he was capable of doing. Once Isa finally made his public appearance, the masses would be so confused as to who was real and who was not, that they dare not put their faith in the Lord anymore.

His time had come and there was no need for pretense. He could show the world his true self…one-eyed and haughty… powerful and seductive. After all, he had world leaders under his wing. He had news teams at his beck-and-call. He had glamorous movie stars and celebrities all willing to do his bidding. The world belonged to him, and no Isa was going to stop him.

Turning to the mirrors at the other end of the room, the Dajjal seethed with anger. He let out a scream from the depths of his ugly soul that rattled the walls and windows. He raised his fists to the sky and shouted, "Isa…you dare to come into *my* world…you dare to challenge me? I am in control here…I gather the people to me with my seductions of fame, wealth, power, and sex. Now, you and I will do battle! We will soon see who prevails!"

With that, the Dajjal's appearance in the mirror, for a brief moment, was that of the bearded man in his fifties, wearing clothing of ancient Jerusalem – his black tunic with the gold belt – his favorite outfit from when he walked the Earth during that period. He smiled an evil smile at himself, and in an instant, was again dressed in modern clothing, his black suit jacket neatly pressed, the hem of his pants just brushing the top of his newly polished shoes. His black tie was smooth against his white shirt, and his black hair neatly groomed. He produced his shiny glass eye from his coat pocket and popped it into its socket. He blinked once, and it became indistinguishable from his good eye.

The world is my chess board. And I am a master player. Humans are my chess pieces – pawns – and sometimes they must be sacrificed.

"Now, Isa, it's time to show the world the monster you really are," he said to his reflection with a bubbling chuckle.

The Dajjal climbed into his high-backed throne-like chair in his office and steepled his fingers. He swiveled the chair to face the massive flatscreen that took up most of one wall and manipulated controls on the remote mounted on the chair's armrest.

Across the entire screen, a multitude of faces appeared in smaller windows, engulfing the expansive monitor. The Dajjal grinned. He knew those under his control had to always be ready whenever he contacted them. Fear of him put him in control. Every one of them had turned to him at some point in the past for help, which he gladly gave. But once received, they were indebted forever and ever. *It was as if they had made a deal with the Devil*, he mused with a grin.

Then there were those leaders he blackmailed for their transgressions against decency. With some it was financial, with some it was sexual, and for some it was many, many things. They were all under his control.

And here they all were, filling his screen with their faces.

"You have all now received information that I've sent electronically. You will release it immediately to the necessary outlets."

Heads bobbed up and down in acknowledgement to his demand. The Dajjal tabbed the controls on his remote and the screen went black. He never let others end the conversation. It was always for him to do. That way he forever remained in control.

*   *   *

A quiet, somber mood hung over Paul, Fatima, and Ali as they stood on the top step in front of the Great Mosque and looked upon the joyous crowd that stretched as far as the eye could see.

"The crowd is growing," Paul said, alarmed. "There's going to be a lot of casualties if there is a military strike."

"We need to find out what's going on around the world," Fatima said. As a journalist, she knew that checking other news sources had a two-fold effect. One, the various news organizations could keep her apprised of what is happening, and two, she could get a good gauge on how the peoples of the world were reacting to that news.

"We can use the news van's satellite uplink to find out," Ali offered.

Fatima nodded and she and Ali started down the steps, leaving Paul behind. She glanced back at him. "Come on."

Paul was pleasantly surprised. "Really?"

"Of course. You were instrumental in getting us in. I'm sure we can help each other out."

Paul smiled and followed them. He enjoyed feeling needed under any circumstance.

With the three of them, the van felt a little cramped, but not so much for Paul. His rarified profession oftentimes stuck him in compromising positions and predicaments. Once they settled in, Ali powered up the satellite dish atop the van and tapped into various news feeds from New York and London. The networks were splayed across several monitors on one wall of the van. One monitor scrolled through a steady stream of news from the internet. Most of the focus was on Abramov, who he was in the world of business, and of the announcement made by the Imam Mahdi. It seemed much of the U.S. scoffed at the idea, though there was extensive discussion among people of faith. There was also a great deal of internet chatter regarding the man who people claimed descended from the sky. The man people claimed to be Isa. Somebody had to bring up the elephant in the room. Paul decided it would be him.

"So, what was – 'Isa' – like?"

"Hard to say. In some respects, he was like anyone else."

"Do you....," Paul let the question trail off. Maybe it's best not to go there.

"Do I what? Believe he is, who he says he is?"

Paul just couldn't bring himself to confirm the question. It was crazy, so he just solemnly nodded.

Fatima looked distressed, uncomfortable in her own skin. "I don't know what to believe anymore," she replied.

"That is usually the first step toward faith," Ali said with a smile.

Paul and Fatima regarded him as one would a mentor or teacher. They both nodded soberly and returned to viewing the monitors receiving various news feeds.

"There are some links about a military buildup in this region. Multiple countries are sending troops and equipment," Fatima said. "Paul, is this a prelude to the airstrike?"

Paul shook his head. "I don't know. I can place a call to the CIA and ask. I still haven't received formal notification that I've lost my credentials and access there, despite Tonklin cutting me out of Glass Eye. I'll try to reach someone."

Ali looked up from a laptop he'd been working with. "Speaking of airstrike, Paul, what's your gut feeling about the timing or if it's going to happen?"

"Oh, it will happen, unless some sort of miracle stops it," he said. The word miracle struck a chord in Fatima and Ali. It didn't go unnoticed in Paul, considering the conversation they just had. He brushed it off and plowed on. "With Abramov in charge – whoever or whatever he is – I think all kinds of hell will break loose. I just don't know where you and I should be when it does. Some things are just completely out of our control, and we have to trust that we'll be in the right place, at the right time. For now, I'm content to continue reading what's out there to figure out how we can help. We probably should book a hotel, too, since it doesn't seem like we're going to be driving back to Jerusalem tonight. Did you two pack any kind of overnight bag?"

Fatima laughed. "Of course, we did. Reporters get used to carrying what's called a 'go bag,' to be ready for all circumstances. A change of clothes is essential. We're good. Sure, we can search for a hotel room online and make reservations from here."

With their night's accommodations in place, Paul stepped out of the van and placed a call to the CIA office. Ali stayed focused on the continuous newsfeeds coming into the van. But Fatima's attention was drawn to Paul as she watched through the dark window. He paced on the sidewalk with his mobile phone pressed to his ear. He sure was handsome, she thought, but she was far more focused on who he was, and what he did for a living. She viewed him as the greater potential story than whatever Ali was following on his monitors.

I wonder if Paul has ever killed anyone. The thought startled her, and she tried to push it away. *Never mind, I don't want to know.*

The look on Paul's face as he came back into the van was serious. "I got through to the CIA offices. They knew nothing about my ties being severed with Glass Eye. For now, I still have access. What I found out is that the military buildup is definitely part of this. Armored military vehicles have been ordered into the streets here in Damascus. They're probably moving into the vicinity of the mosque as we speak. We can expect that military choppers will be flying overhead during the night, and ships from Europe have been redirected to the Suez Canal. It's all in preparation for whatever the airstrike will entail and the fallout from it. What I'm not sure about is how much of it is being ordered by the world's governments, and what of it is being directed by Abramov's puppets. Intelligence is still being gathered. And complicating matters, TRIAD activity has escalated throughout the world. I guess they're taking advantage of the situation by striking while the world's intelligence agencies are distracted by the events here in Damascus."

Fatima and Ali looked at each other, then turned to Paul. "Well, at least we know something," Ali said. "While I don't want to be at the mosque when any bombs are dropped, I don't want to be accused of being a coward, if I ask for us to go to our hotel."

"You're right, Ali," Fatima said. "There's not much we can do at this point. The Imam was warned. This is bigger than all of us. If something falls from the sky, I don't want to be where it lands, either."

"Then let's head to the hotel and get settled in," Paul said. He didn't want to tell Fatima and Ali that there were rumors spreading through the world's governments, that this so-called Isa was a terrorist and his descent from the sky was an elaborate hoax. He thought they should have time to sleep and clear their heads before jumping into the next world upheaval. Maybe he was just being selfish. He, too, needed some sleep and would have a new perspective in the morning.

Fatima and Ali drove behind Paul as he led them the few blocks to the hotel.

"What do you think is happening at *News World*?" Ali asked.

"You were monitoring their feed, so you know."

"Sure, they were reporting basically the same thing as every other station, but you know what I mean. Christopher Munson always looks to push the news a little further than other networks. I'm just wondering what's going on behind the scenes."

"Yeah, you're right," Fatima said with a sly smile. "Christopher is always looking for a different perspective that other news agencies overlook."

Ali took his gaze off the road and looked at her. He could tell something was up. "What's going on, Fatima?"

"I sent him an email," Fatima said as she absently stared out the window at the passing buildings and Syrian citizens.

"Did you fill him in on what's going on?"

"I did better than that," she smirked.

"What do you mean?"

"Let's just say I did my job as a journalist. And I think it's going to stir up a hornet's nest."

Ali blinked several times, not knowing what to say.

*   *   *

It was late night at the *News World* offices in New York City, yet the place still bustled with activity because the news never sleeps.

Christopher sat in his office, bleary-eyed from a long day, staring at his desktop computer screen. On it was a grouping of screenshots of Abramov's party taken from the camera sewn in the clutch Fatima took to the party. It was attached to an email sent by Fatima, from Damascus. The email contained a detailed account of her unauthorized, and undercover, sojourn to Abramov's party, facilitated with the help of an unnamed CIA agent. She danced around the issue of exactly what happened, spinning it as Abramov running more of a criminal empire involving the world's elite, as opposed to him being an evil spiritual entity that's been alive forever and hellbent on destroying the world and collecting its souls. Sure, it wasn't quite the truth, but, most importantly, she needed to let

Munson know at least some of the truth about Abramov – that he was not to be trusted and was more dangerous than a typical corporate raider. She insisted he start an investigation into everything Richard Abramov has been involved in his entire life. Though she challenged Munson to find anything about Abramov on the internet. She knew that would light a fire in Christopher and he'd leverage all his journalistic resources to find something, anything, about Abramov. And if she even hinted, that she thought, they were dealing with the Antichrist, Munson would ignore everything else and focus solely on that. He'd consider it nonsense and label her mentally unstable.

Her gamble paid off.

At 8 p.m., Christopher Munson called an emergency meeting with all his department heads and officially launched an investigation into the life of Richard Abramov. No stone was to be left unturned.

The meeting had barely got underway when a young, eager production assistant poked her head into the room.

"Mr. Munson?"

"Yes," Chris said with a little more impatience than he intended. His long day was getting longer, and it was starting to show. "I'm sorry, what is it?"

"We received information on the identity of the man in the mosque in Damascus. The one that supposedly arrived from the sky."

A few in the room chuckled, letting everyone know what they thought of that story.

"Where did the info come from?" Chris asked.

The production assistant stepped into the room, holding a printout that was several pages long.

"It appears to be from the FBI. All the major, news media outlets around the world have received the same info from various intelligence services."

Christopher took the printout from her and started reading.

CHAPTER SIXTEEN

Tonklin rode in a jeep through the dusty streets of Damascus beneath an ink black sky. He was heading toward the base camp of other military vehicles, to prepare for the assault on the Great Mosque.

His jeep was escorted by a troop transport in case any of the more dangerous locals decided to open fire on them. Tonklin half-hoped they would. Nothing like a good firefight to release the building tension he felt. He really just wanted to get on with the attack and be done with it. This waiting drove him crazy.

His cell phone vibrated, and he jumped. *Must be more on edge than I thought.* He snatched the phone from his waistband. It was a text from Abramov. It only contained GPS coordinate numbers. Tonklin stared at the numbers, perplexed, when Abramov called him.

He answered but before he could speak, the caller interrupted.

"Tonklin." The voice was loud in the phone speaker; there was something unearthly about Abramov's tone. A sound like a snake's hiss weaved its way through the voice. A cold chill rushed down Tonklin's spine, and for the first time since he began working for Abramov, he felt uneasy.

"Yes, sir!" Tonklin replied, trying to mask his discomfort.

Abramov either didn't notice or didn't care. "I want you to fire an artillery shell at the coordinates I just texted you."

Excitement bubbled up in Tonklin, regardless of how talking to his boss made him feel. "So, this begins our airstrike?"

"No. This is just a prelude. I want the shell fired low, beneath radar."

"I... don't understand."

An explosion of anger from the phone. "It's not your place to understand, Tonklin! Your place is to follow my orders! I expect the shell to be fired immediately, and for the attack not to be traced back to you. If it's traced to you then it might be traced to me. And I would be very put out."

The phone went dead. Tonklin fumbled it back onto the clasp at his waist. Even with the cool wind blowing through the jeep, Tonklin was coated in sweat.

✻   ✻   ✻

Fatima woke from a deep sleep at the sound of an explosion. She ran to the window and looked in the direction of the Great Mosque. No fires, nothing flying overhead. She quickly threw on some clothes, grabbed her cell phone, and called Paul as she ran across the hallway and pounded on Ali's hotel room door.

"Ali, quick, did you hear that noise?" Ali opened the door before she finished asking the question.

"Yes, yes, we need to get to the mosque. Where's Paul?" he asked as he finished tucking in his shirt.

"I'm calling him now." Before the phone finished three rings, Paul ran out of the door of his room, located at the other end of the hall. He sprinted toward the pair.

"I need to get to the mosque," he said, as he hurried to the elevator.

"We're going with you!" Fatima shouted.

"Yeah! And I need to grab my gear!" Ali added, dashing back into his hotel room.

Paul sighed impatiently and waited for them. They were civilians and he was concerned for their safety. Even so, they helped him get into the mosque and let him sit in their van while they accessed the world's news feeds through their satellite link. That gave him some intel and insight into what was happening around the world.

A few minutes later they were in Paul's car, speeding to the Great Mosque.

"What did you think of that boom?" Fatima asked Paul. "Without seeing any fires or more artillery, I'm not sure what we heard."

Paul shook his head. "I don't know."

"Could it be the airstrike?" Ali asked.

"Probably not. That would be a sustained attack. Not a single explosion. And the sky would be filled with military jets."

"But can you be certain?" Fatima asked, not sure if she wanted to hear the answer.

"I don't know," Paul said solemnly.

They rounded a corner, a block from the mosque. Thousands of people were still there in the streets, all staring into the distance, away from the mosque. Paul, Fatima, and Ali simultaneously looked at the mosque, and were relieved to see it was still standing and appeared completely unscathed.

They followed the gaze of the onlookers. It led deeper into the city where thick smoke furled visibly, even against the black sky.

Paul drove his car as close as he could before the crowd was too dense to continue. He parked, and they got out.

Ali immediately perched his camera on his shoulder, pointed the lens at the smoke and began recording.

"I wonder what happened?" Fatima asked, to no one in particular.

"A missile just flew over, only a few hundred feet above us," a tall, lanky man with glasses said. "It came out of nowhere."

Paul and Fatima exchanged concerned looks. His CIA-trained instincts kicked in and he started sprinting toward the explosion site. Fatima pounded the pavement after him. Ali joined them, struggling to keep his camera secure on his shoulder and recording.

Fatima and Ali ran several blocks, trying to keep up with Paul. But he was in excellent shape, courtesy of the American taxpayer.

He came upon the scene first, then they stumbled in behind him. It was carnage. Dead, burnt bodies smoldered in the street. The fronts of the surrounding buildings were caved in. Horrifying.

Ali stepped up with his camera and worked the focus ring.

"Ali! Maybe you shouldn't!" Paul said, alarmed.

"It's what we do, Paul," Fatima responded. Her voice was remarkably calm.

Her cell phone rang, a little too loudly. It was Christopher Munson calling. "Yes, Chris."

"What the hell is going on over there? Are you two all right?" he shouted into her ear. The rising panic in his voice was unmistakable.

"We don't know yet. We are on the scene of a military strike. Dead bodies are everywhere."

"Then you need to get away from there, now!"

"Relax, Chris, we're fine," she said as she turned away from the scene. Fatima was used to being in intense situations as the networks foreign correspondent in the Middle East but had never seen the immediate aftermath of an explosion that resulted in death. However, she didn't want Munson to be overly worried. Especially since there was nothing he could do about it, being thousands of miles away.

"Were you able to look into Richard Abramov yet? He might be the one behind this attack."

"Forget him. I just got word from our government contacts that they believe the strike came from the mosque, purposely killing a bunch of Christians. An attack directed by this guy claiming to be Jesus, or Isa, or whatever."

"That's crazy, Chris. The mosque has no weapons, and there are Christians among those here. The Imam welcomes them with open arms. And the Jews too."

"Nonetheless, that's what I've been told. It's heating up fast and I fear for your and Ali's safety."

She turned back to the carnage and just stared at the dead bodies without blinking.

Chris's voice echoed in her ear. "Fatima? Fatima?"

Could it be true? Could this so-called Isa be a terrorist?

✶   ✶   ✶

Fatima pounded on the magnificent doors of the Umayyad Mosque – the Great Mosque of Damascus. It was the middle of the night, and the doors were locked, but she didn't care. She wanted answers and she gave no mind to the hour, nor to the disrespect her behavior showed to the ancient and revered structure. Paul and Ali stood behind her, with thousands of people behind them. She continued pounding with no signs of tiring. She was a journalist on a mission and – by God – no one was getting in her way. She had ended her call with Christopher under the pretense that she was losing the cell signal. Chris didn't particularly sound like he bought it – it was such a clichéd trick – but she didn't care. Fatima needed to get off the phone and get to her task. And here she was.

Pound – pound – pound.

She heard someone working the metal latch on the inside. Pieces of ancient metal protested as they scraped against each other. She stepped back. After what seemed like an eternity, one of the two doors creaked open. Jamal poked his head out.

"I need to see Isa right now," Fatima demanded without hesitation.

Jamal sighed with exhaustion. "Now is not the right time."

"I spoke to my superior and have been told that my government thinks this mosque is harboring terrorists," she said. Then, in a softer tone, "Please, I need to speak to Isa. I might be able to help the situation."

Jamal sighed again as he considered her words. After a moment, he opened the door wider to let her pass. Fatima entered, followed by Paul and Ali. The two men made sure to stay close to Fatima, so as not to be shut out of the mosque. It was unnecessary, as Jamal didn't try to keep them out.

Jamal led the way with a flashlight. It was an interesting contrast. An oil lantern or a torch would've been more appropriate. The mosque was more than thirteen hundred years old and although it had been restored repeatedly over the centuries, it still maintained its elegant and traditional architecture. Fatima marveled at the grand hallway and the marble pillars. It truly was like strolling from the present into the ancient past.

They arrived at the Imam's office. Jamal turned to Fatima and the others and raised a finger to his lips. Respectively, they went silent. He slowly opened the door to the office and poked his head in. Inside, Imam Mahdi quietly conferred with Isa.

"I'm sorry to interrupt, but there are visitors with an urgent message," Jamal said.

"We know," Isa said. There was no egotism or braggadocio in his demeanor. He spoke with a relaxed and understanding tone.

"Should we come back another time?" Jamal asked.

"No, that is okay, Jamal, they may enter," Isa said in a teacher-like manner.

Jamal opened the door all the way and motioned the others inside. Fatima swiftly stepped in like a pushy journalist. Ali dutifully stepped off to her side, and slightly behind her, as he had done a hundred times before. Paul, usually the more assertive one, shrank into the background keeping a respectable distance, more out of embarrassment than anything. His natural instinct was to disbelieve in the returning Messiah, but he had become open-minded enough to consider there are aspects of the universe which defied his understanding or preconceived notions.

Ali's camera shut off with an audible whine, as if the battery had suddenly died. Fatima glanced back at him as he shrugged in confusion.

"The camera isn't necessary at this time, Ali," Isa said calmly.

Fatima tried to hide her surprise at Isa knowing Ali's camera failed – *did he cause it?* – as well as him knowing Ali's name. Maybe his name was mentioned at the earlier meeting, but she couldn't remember for certain. She shook it off as irrelevant and forged ahead.

"Isa," she began, feeling a little odd in case she misjudged who he claimed to be, "my boss in the United States has informed me that many of the world's nations view you as a terrorist, who just fired a missile into a crowd of people. Do you have any comment on that?" She couldn't help herself. She would forever be a journalist.

"Yes, Fatima, I have a comment – many comments in fact. And I want to say them to the whole world. As they say in your lexicon... I'll give you an exclusive."

She was surprised at his knowledge of her field and his contemporariness in general.

"But first... feel free to check the mosque for any military equipment that might suggest we fired the missile. I grant you access to all parts, but you will find none."

Fatima glanced back at Paul. He perked up. Finally, something for him to do that utilizes his expertise. He gladly left the room.

Isa returned to the business at hand. "Now, contact Mr. Munson and set up the broadcast as soon as possible. Would you do that for me?" His smile was so warm and genuine, his voice so full of truth and reason, it touched her very soul. She wondered how she could have doubted him in the first place.

"Yes, Isa, I'll contact him right away." She gave a quick curtsy, something unlike her, but it felt right in the moment.

"Thank you. He's been trying to reach you for the last few minutes, but your phone is shut off."

"Yes, it is," she said, giving him a knowing smile.

*   *   *

Fatima dropped her purse and laptop on the bed in the hotel room. She was relieved when Paul reported back that there wasn't a trace of military equipment of any kind in the mosque. No weapons at all, in fact. Not so much as a handgun. She was exhausted but couldn't crawl into bed until she talked with Munson in New York. She placed the call. Munson picked it up on the third ring.

"Fatima! Where are you? I've been trying to reach you since we got disconnected!" he said.

"Yes, I know… Isa told me," she laughed.

"What did you say? Isa told you?" Munson sounded severely confused. He rose from his desk and poured a cup of coffee. His tie was loose around his collar, and he was tired.

"It's real, Christopher. He's here…I know in my heart, it's him." She took off her shoes and rubbed her feet on the soft carpet as she talked.

"Fatima, have you been drinking?"

Fatima laughed. "No, haven't had a drop of alcohol, Chris. You should know better than to even ask me that. And tomorrow morning, we're going to broadcast his message to the world, Ali and me and you. That's why I'm calling. You need to set this up on your end. It's daytime there, just about midnight here. We can get it on tomorrow night's broadcast. Isa will speak at the Great Mosque here in Damascus. There are thousands of people still camped out, on the steps, on the streets. They answered the Imam's call for peace, and it's real."

Munson thought for a minute before replying. "Fatima, I don't believe you've talked to Isa. Or as some would call him – Jesus. I'm sorry, I just don't believe it, because I don't believe Isa exists. He's just a story in an ancient book. A fairy tale. That being said, I'd be more than happy to interview this man who claims he's Isa since much of the world views him as a terrorist. I'd have to clear it with the higher-ups, but they would probably agree that this person who calls himself Isa is definitely newsworthy. But I've received other intel from the FBI that I need to verify first, before I do anything."

"What intel?"

"I can't discuss it now. Not until I learn more," Christopher said. He knew that wouldn't sit well with Fatima, but he enjoyed having the upper hand for a change.

"Okay. Do whatever you need to do to get this on the air." She ended the call before he could say anything else.

Munson stood there, staring at his phone.

The world has gone completely insane.

CHAPTER SEVENTEEN

The sun rose the next morning amidst a paint-brushed pink and blue sky of whimsical clouds and birds flying overhead. The people remained on the steps and streets outside the Umayyad Mosque. Blankets and food had been distributed by the staffs of nearby churches, synagogues, and by the mosque workers.

On the roof of buildings a few blocks away, heavily armed men from Glass Eye surveyed the area around the mosque. A lieutenant spotted several news trucks in the vicinity, with media people interviewing various individuals from the crowd. News helicopters circled overhead. Miles away, black military vehicles, jeeps, troop transports, and trucks with large caliber guns mounted on them were staged, their engines on idle, men with machine guns wandering aimlessly among the trucks. On the sides of the vehicles, the name of Glass Eye Global Security was clearly marked.

David Tonklin, seated in a jeep, grabbed his ringing cell phone.

"Tonklin here."

"Sir, the people appear to be completely unarmed."

"Good, just the way we like it," Tonklin said. He tapped his hand on the steering wheel.

"But, sir, the media is everywhere. The entire world is watching. We may have to call this off," the lieutenant said.

"Dammit. I need to make a call. Stand down, until you hear from me." Tonklin ended the call before making another. "I need to talk to Abramov. It's Tonklin."

*   *   *

Fatima woke as the first ray of sunlight shone in through the window. She texted Ali and Paul, then hopped into the shower.

The three had agreed to meet at the hotel breakfast bar to grab juice, fruit, and some toast before heading to the mosque. In the car, seated in the back, Fatima placed a call to Munson as the two men conversed in the front seat.

"Chris, we're on our way to the mosque with our cameras. Do you have the broadcast coordinates in place?" She jumped right in, not waiting for his hello.

"Working on it, Fatima," Munson said.

"Look, Christopher, we should be set and ready to go within the hour. We know Isa plans to come outside to talk to the people, and we want to give him a worldwide audience. This is history!"

He hesitated. "Yeah, I know. He's the Muslim Messiah. Only I grew up to believe in other things, Fatima. I will do what I can. Let me know when you're ready to go live." He ended the call.

They pulled up to the back entrance to the mosque, and the guards waved them through. Ali parked the car, and they got out; he retrieved the camera equipment, and they headed up the stairs.

Paul had noticed additional military trucks parked a couple of blocks away, as they neared the mosque, and let Fatima and Ali know.

They got to the terrace and decided to set up the cameras just outside the front door, figuring that was the spot from where Isa would address the crowd. The people remained peaceful and were encouraged to know that the Imam would soon speak to them. Their spirits were high even after the inexplicable attack last night that struck several blocks away. They were just excited that Isa was among them, and each person hoped to have time to talk with him, or at least to try.

Inside the mosque, the Imam and Jamal had worked out the morning's logistics with Isa. They were just heading out to the front of the mosque when Paul, Fatima, and Ali hurried up to them. Fatima and Ali greeted Isa in a respectful manner. Paul kept to a professional demeanor and just nodded toward Isa and the Imam.

"Good morning, Isa," Fatima said. "We have our cameras set up outside near the front entry doors."

Paul stepped up. "Gentlemen, there has been a military build-up overnight, so you need to be quick with this broadcast. I fear—"

Isa raised his hand. "What will happen, will happen. Do not be afraid, Paul. You have a good heart. I know you have always tried to do the right thing. I have seen you in your days and in your nights. Today will be okay. Trust me."

Paul was left with nothing to say. He nodded and backed away to let Isa pass.

Isa stopped in front of Fatima. "As for you, Fatima, don't doubt yourself. Trust me. I know it's difficult, considering how your uncle treated you. But know that the ways of man will often lead one astray, even those claiming to follow a faith. Though you have lost your faith, you've still called out to Allah, and he has heard you, and gave you strength. Look at what you have accomplished in life. Your strength has made you the woman you are now."

His words left her stunned and silent. She felt tears well up in her throat. She felt reassured and reminiscent. But she had a show to do, and those thoughts must wait for another time. She looked at Paul, who smiled at her and led her outside where the cameras stood waiting.

Ali was in touch with Munson, connected via his earpiece. "We're good to go! I'll do the countdown when we're ready to start. Isa should be out here in a couple minutes."

Christopher Munson sat behind his anchor desk with a heavy heart. He couldn't bring himself to tell Fatima or Ali that the higher-ups brought him an FBI report detailing that while a man claiming to be Isa descended from the sky in the Middle East, it was in reality, a giant hoax. There was much more damning information and Christopher was about to go live on the air with it. This was the price of putting on an exclusive interview with Isa. It was the official disclaimer.

Even under the bright studio lights, Munson saw the "on air" sign light up and began his report.

"Several days ago, a man appeared in Damascus, seemingly coming from the sky. Some people claim this man to be Jesus. And some call him by his Islamic name, Isa. Either way, these same people claim we are now living amid the Second Coming."

Alongside Munson appeared images of the Umayyad Mosque and grainy amateur footage of Isa's decent from the sky.

"Our own intelligence agencies, such as the FBI, along with those of other governments around the world, have corroborated the news. But this man's appearance from the sky has been confirmed to be a hoax accomplished with digital video trickery. Intelligence agencies have identified this man as Barabbas Absalom, a criminal from Jerusalem, and the possible leader of TRIAD. They say he is responsible for orchestrating many terrorist group activities around the globe, regardless of cultural or religious affiliations. Including the destruction of the Al-Aqsa Mosque and the Dome of the Rock in Jerusalem. As well as the attack that took the lives of more than a hundred people yesterday."

Ali caught the last minute of the broadcast, stunned at Munson's words. Fatima saw it on his face. "What is it, Ali?"

His voice cracked with emotion. "Munson just betrayed us and all that's about to happen, telling lies about Isa, and now the entire world has heard it, all lies."

Ali quickly tapped a couple switches so Fatima could hear what Munson was saying.

People watching the news around the world were in shock. Munson's program was not only broadcasted live in the U.S. but also on affiliate stations in Canada and the U.K. Furthermore, due to the significance of the broadcast, it was allowed to be aired on stations across most of the world. Viewers who tuned in to hear a message from Isa were instead informed that he was a fake and a terrorist.

Christopher took a deep breath and continued. "We've been told his sudden public appearance now, complete with an outlandish, over-the-top mode of entrance has many governments alarmed."

In the van, Ali stared at the monitor and listened to Christopher while Fatima listened in despair through her earpiece as he went on. "Intelligence reports reveal he's amassing a large army with a cache of WMDs that might include nuclear weapons. This is a developing story, and we will keep you apprised of more information as we learn it."

As Fatima heard Christopher sign off in her earpiece, she boiled with anger.

"I can't believe Christopher is buying this," she said.

"Christopher doesn't believe he's Isa. He's an agnostic at best."

"I realize that. But to assume he's a terrorist is a stretch. Ali, what do we do now? We're about to go live in less than five minutes!" She looked for Paul, who stood near the entry doors at the top of the stairs. He was unaware of what had just happened in New York, not having an earpiece as she and Ali did. She waved him over to where she stood and filled him in on what was transpiring.

"Your boss believing Isa is a terrorist might not be quite the stretch you think," Paul said.

"What do you mean?"

"Since Richard Abramov owns Glass Eye Global Security and the CIA loaned me out to them, I'm sure Abramov has the resources and influence to leak fake information to implicate Isa as a terrorist. In fact, I'm sure he's done just that. It's just a matter of time now, until the world's militaries mobilize for some form of assault on the mosque."

The thought sent a chill through Fatima.

In the meantime, the crowd on the staircase and spread out along the streets waited in anticipation. They had been there for two days to hear the uniting words of Imam Mahdi and the unexpected surprise of Isa's arrival.

Paul was ready to help. "Let me get Jamal…we'll talk with Isa." He ran to the entry doors and the guards let him inside.

Jamal was just down the hall, waiting outside of the Imam's office, as Paul hurried up to him and said, "Jamal, something terrible has happened in the worldwide media stream. They are spreading lies about Isa, and I need to talk to him."

Jamal nodded and knocked on the door, and the Imam said, "Come in."

The Imam and Isa sat in chairs next to the curtained window. They watched the TV screen on a station where Munson was just finishing his broadcast.

"So, you know what he's said about you today?" Paul asked. "I should have known."

"It's okay, Paul," Isa said calmly, reaching out his hands. "It's not the first time people have spread lies about who I am and what I represent. It will be all right."

The Imam and Jamal listened quietly. They knew the people outside were getting anxious for some news and prayers from the Imam.

Paul stood before Isa. "Sir, is there anything I can do to help?"

Isa nodded, a wide smile on his face. "Yes. Bring me a laptop computer."

Paul grinned with surprise at the request. This man – Isa – was supposed to be about two thousand years old, which was difficult enough for Paul to wrap his mind around, but to hear him speak with ease in 21st century terms, fully understanding this world of technology that he was now present in astounded Paul.

"Right away, sir," Paul said.

That was another thing that amazed him. Isa commanded respect. Not from intimidation or threat, but just because of his very presence. The peace and love in him pulled the respect out of people. At least most people, Paul surmised. Surely there are people whose hearts were so corrupt that even Isa's presence had no effect.

Tonklin is probably one of those. The sudden thought startled Paul, and he pushed it out of his mind.

Paul connected outside with Ali, who provided him with a laptop. Before going back inside, Paul reassured Fatima that Isa had things under control. He took the laptop to Isa, who signed on to the device. *Where is he going with this?* Paul thought.

Unbeknownst to Paul, and most of the world, Tonklin had reached Abramov and after a very uncomfortable conversation – for Tonklin, not for Abramov – in which Tonklin apprised Abramov of their current situation involving a massive media buildup outside the Great Mosque, Richard Abramov knew exactly what to do. He ended the conversation abruptly. No need for pleasantries with Tonklin. Though the ex-military man was one of the Dajjal's more skilled and useful minions, there's no reason to cut him anymore slack than he would with anyone else. Tonklin, after all, was just another human being with a relatively short lifespan, like all the individuals the Dajjal encountered during his numerous travels. They would serve him, perish, and then be replaced by others.

The Dajjal made a call to the Syrian Presidential Palace.

"This is Richard Abramov. Put him on," he said when an aide answered the phone.

The aide didn't need to know who the "him" in the sentence was referring to. When Richard Abramov called, it was always to speak to the Syrian President. And the President had standing instructions that he was to be summoned whenever Abramov called. No matter what. Whether he was in a meeting, giving a press conference, sleeping or in the shower. He stopped what he was doing and answered Abramov's call.

Within seconds he was on the phone.

"What can I do for you, Mr. Abramov?" he asked with a slight quiver in his voice.

The Dajjal's mouth stretched into an inhuman grin. If the president could see it, his heart might fail from fright. But though he couldn't see him, he was still afraid of Abramov. Most people were. And the Dajjal loved it. It was one of the few things he did love.

"Here's what I need you to do…," he began.

*   *   *

The control room at *News World* was in chaos. Munson shouted orders to the technicians and the producer.

"What do you mean there's a media blackout?" Munson shouted. "I was just on the air! We're ready for Fatima's report! Has the network's AI system gone down?"

The producer stepped back to be out of Munson's hitting distance. "No, sir. The IT department checked the Artificial Intelligence system immediately, and it's operating properly. It's due to the Syrian president. He just ordered all media out of the country."

Munson held his head in his hands. "This can't be happening!"

A production assistant stepped up to Munson's desk. "Sir, there's a video call for you. He's on now," she said, pointing to the screen behind him.

"Who…what…?" He turned around to see the face of Isa. "What is this, a joke?"

"Hello, Christopher," Isa said. "You'll find that this call is real, as am I."

"He's right, Mr. Munson," the producer said. "Our IT guys say the signal is originating from Damascus."

Munson stared speechless at the image on the screen. The man looked so kind, harmless, loving. *That can't be*, he thought. "How can I help you, sir…Mr. Absalom…Isa?"

"I'm going to make an announcement to the world. We have the cameras set up here at the Great Mosque, with your team of Fatima and Ali. You have the communications infrastructure. We're going to send our signal to your Middle Eastern satellite. You just need to be sure the signal is live and gets sent…everywhere. You can do that, can't you?" His voice was gentle but firm.

Munson was silent. The producer nudged his arm. Still no response to Isa's question.

"Mr. Munson…Christopher…you know I can do this without you, don't you?"

"You really could, couldn't you?" Munson said sheepishly. He could see it in the man's eyes. Though he was sincere, honest, and peaceful, he commanded great power. No, not commanded. He was supported by great power. It was invisible but it was unmistakably there. Always present. Never tiring. And although Christopher Munson didn't want to think about it, he understood that power was infinite.

Isa nodded. "Yes, yes, I can."

Munson relented, "Okay, I'll do what you ask. Tell Fatima and Ali to stand by."

Isa ended the video call.

CHAPTER EIGHTEEN

Tonklin sat in his jeep, stationed at the city limits of Damascus, watching the news on a tablet. He knew Abramov intended for this airstrike to happen despite anything Isa might do. As if he'd read his mind, the caller ID on his cell phone showed Abramov was calling. Tonklin answered it on the first ring.

"Yes, sir. We're ready if you are. It's a go then!" Tonklin waved at his men who stood outside their vehicles, waiting for the word.

Out on the Mediterranean Sea, warships from multiple countries moved toward Syria. In the air above them flew fighter jets. On the outskirts of the city, tanks, jeeps, and transport vehicles moved forward in a caravan, headed for Damascus.

At the Great Mosque, Fatima and Ali were ready to begin the broadcast. She had notified Munson that the Imam and Isa would be out in about five minutes. The crowd was more than ready to hear their holy words. She attached her microphone to her lapel and adjusted her earpiece. Ali stood ready at the cameras. He had them set up at various locations, knowing the producers in the control room would choose from the two angles at various times.

Paul looked out over the crowd and noticed in the distance a line of tanks and other military vehicles moving slowly toward the center of the city. Fear rose in his stomach as he worried what would happen if the tanks arrived before Isa finished talking. Would Tonklin and Abramov actually attempt to murder Isa and all these people while they were on the air?

At last, the giant double doors of the mosque opened, and out into the sun stepped Imam Mahdi, his assistant Jamal – and Isa. The people cheered and clapped. Though the world had a particular image of what Isa looked like in their minds, he shook up expectations by wearing modern-day clothing, his hair and beard groomed in a contemporary style. Isa was not tied to a specific era or location. He existed outside space and time and fit in wherever he chose to appear.

On the broadcast from New York, Munson gave an introduction. "Today, the entire world will hear from a man who says he is Isa, or Jesus as the Christians refer to him, returned to Earth after two thousand years. Earlier in the day, we announced what intelligence reports said, that this man is instead a terrorist who goes by the name of Barabbas Absalom. Who is he really? You will have to judge for yourselves. Does he intend to make a threat? Demands? Give us a warning? We don't know.

"This broadcast is being aired worldwide," Munson continued, "and people will have the privilege of hearing his announcement. We have a reporter and cameraman on the ground at the mosque in Damascus, who are feeding the video and audio to all other news stations via our technology at *News World*. Fatima, are you ready to begin?"

She nodded to Isa, who stood at the microphone placed in front of the mosque's entryway, and to Ali, who was ready behind the camera. Out of the corner of her eye, she saw Paul; the worried look on his face concerned her.

The people stopped talking as Isa stepped closer to the microphone.

In the distance, the military vehicles moved closer to the mosque, about one mile away now. Paul continued to watch their progress and wondered what he could do to stop them.

The cameras focused on Isa's radiant smile as he scanned the crowd from right to left, capturing everyone's attention. Behind him, large projection screens made it easy for the people standing on the streets to see his face. Large speakers were placed to project his words.

"Good day, people of the world. There has been much talk around the globe today as to who I am. Much of what was reported was false, a lie. My name is not Barabbas Absalom. First, I will tell you who I am not: I am not a terrorist. I am not commanding armies of terrorists, nor am I amassing a stockpile of weapons. I have not come to make demands nor to destroy your lives. My name is Isa, and I have come so that you might live in peace. I have not come to wage war against the people of the world.

"I have come to bring peace to the Earth. And understanding, not just between myself and all your religions, but between each other. Regardless of what you believe in terms of faith or politics, we are all the same."

People from around the world were tuned into the broadcast. The president of the United States was watching from the Oval Office. The heads of state in Russia watched from the Kremlin. The emperor of China watched on his laptop computer. From France, Scotland, England, Germany, Switzerland, the Baltic states, Africa, Australia, and Indonesia…people watched.

"You have seen so-called miracles performed by a man named Richard Abramov. He has many powerful people under his spell. He has used trickery to create events to get the world to believe in him. He is indeed the Dajjal, the Antichrist, and he was alive during my first time on Earth…he has affected many events throughout history, and today he stands ready to destroy mankind.

"Some will love me for saying that about him; others will hate me. Some won't care. But I care…deeply…about each and every one of you! Many religious scholars will question who I am. They read the Torah, the Bible, the Qur'an, the Buddhist Tipitaka, the Hindu Bhagavad Gita. I am as human as you are. I was when I walked the Earth more than two thousand years ago! And I am human now."

Isa asked Jamal for a drink of water because he was thirsty. Jamal obliged, and Isa continued with his talk.

"See, I thirst. I eat food. I walk, talk and can dance…if the music is right." The crowd laughed at this.

Overhead the noise of military choppers sounded, and the crowd grew nervous.

"At this moment," Isa continued, "much of the world's military might is descending on Damascus – because of me. It is not my wish to cause bloodshed! As it states in the Qur'an, 'But they plan and Allah plans. And Allah is the best of planners.'

"The Christians of the world will question why I quote from the Qur'an. It carries the same messages the Bible does. 'Many are the plans in a person's heart, but it is the Lord's purpose that prevails.' See – different words, but the same meaning, the latter being from Proverbs. The Jews will ask, 'Why are you not mentioned in the Torah?' Because the five books of the Torah were revealed before I was born! I am the Isa of all the holy books. I am that Isa without the mention of whom no Holy Book is complete. The Christians or the Bible do not hold monopoly on me just as no one holds a monopoly over air, sunlight, rain, happiness, or sorrow.

"I look out over this crowd gathered here, and I see humans…different colors, different races. I see Christians, Jews, Muslims – all holding hands, praying together. You three are the faiths descended from Abraham – do you not realize this? You are the same in your hearts, but you don't remember this. Instead, there is division and hate. That is not my message – my message is one of love. Love each other. Be at peace."

The military vehicles surrounded the mosque and the people on all sides. The crowd grew nervous, and some at the edges of the streets ran away, not staying for the rest of Isa's message.

He continued, despite the presence of tanks. "Our war on Earth has never been against one particular religion, place of worship, or a person. It has always been against Satan, who believes that he is superior to Adam. He has used the weak mentality and concealed emotions of human beings to prove his superiority. When the truth is told in the world, hatred is banished and there should be no war. We should solve our problems using logic and arguments, not weapons.

"I will turn myself over to any authority figures to avoid any conflict. There is no need for shots to be fired. No need for people to suffer injury or incarceration. If you are concerned because of me, then take me, and only me."

The noise from the choppers flying overhead seemed to drown out his words, but the technicians turned up the volume as Isa continued.

"Some have asked me to prove who I am. Should I show you a miracle to make you believe? Should I pause the world with my finger? Should I open a window in the sky?"

Fatima wondered if Isa was going to do just that. She hoped Ali would capture it on video if a window were suddenly to open above.

"Some will ask why God in heaven offers some people gifts, which others in life do not get. Why does He do that? So that the Lord God can see if each one thanks him for their blessings or if it only escalates a person's pride. This is how He has crafted the universe -- judging some by giving to them and others by taking from them. He does this, so that on the Day of Judgment he can reward those who were able to comprehend the simple concept that nothing in this universe happens without the consent of the Almighty! So that He can punish the ungrateful individuals who were not able to understand such a simple concept while living in this mighty universe. I stand before you today, people of the world, to help you understand that every discussion, every decision you make will ultimately lead towards God or his message. Or towards death, or the Hereafter."

The crowd hung on to his every word. People around the globe watching from their homes wept. Those viewing the scene on TV sets in shopping malls were silent, and stood together in peace and harmony, listening, and believing that this man on the screen was indeed Isa, and that they were witnessing his Second Coming.

"God in Heaven is more interested in attracting mankind towards Him than I am. He who gave life and gave humans incredible brains to think with. He who gave them empathetic hearts to feel. That praiseworthy God who filled my heart with love and affection for entire generations of mankind. He who has blessed every inch of the Earth with His miracles and creations. He would want nothing, except that humans would reflect upon His creations and miracles, propagate the purity of their God, and enlighten each other with His Greatness. Loving, supporting, and helping each other in life.

Even Pharaoh ventured out to establish peace in the world, with Haman, the leader of the learned, and with Qaroon, the leader of the wealthy. Instead, God gave Moses a stick and sent him to prevent Pharaoh from spreading mischief on land. The attempts at peace are analogous to that of someone who gives in to his desire and not that of someone who submits to the will of his Creator."

The military vehicles slowed and stopped, as the soldiers turned off their engines. The choppers flew to a location a few miles away. All the weapons that had been trained on Isa from rooftops were lowered. In Washington, D.C. and the Kremlin, the two world leaders spoke by phone. Members of Parliament in Israel waited to hear from Prime Minister Nicholas Wilder; he called to tell them to order the Israeli troops to stand down. The crowd gathered at the mosque noticed the vehicles backing off, and the people broke into a loud cheer.

"God's blessings to humanity are all around you. The billions and billions of stars in the sky. The beauty of the rising and setting sun. The moon that waxes and wanes to help you count the days. And most of all, the miracle of the transformation of a tiny drop of human fluid to combine with the cells in the womb of a woman to form a living human being that will grow inside of her. Such as the fact that a universe exists in everything from a mosquito to the planets and heavens above. Humans have witnessed the miracles within the Earth, such as crude oil and minerals beneath its surface. And in today's world, humanity has not entered this technologically advanced age solely by their own actions, but because mankind was predestined to reach this stage."

The people at the mosque listened without moving. They had never before heard such instruction and such intelligence.

"I will talk now about the extremist religious groups, such as TRIAD, and all others who assume they have the right to shed blood of anyone they wish to kill. They want to demolish the worship places of every religion except their own, the ones who forcibly want to make others follow their ideologies. Hear this: they are wrong. They are trapped in darkness and ignorance, which can only be eliminated by lighting the lamp of knowledge. There is no other way. A God who, had he allowed compulsion in religion, would have done so through the swing of his first prophet's fingers.

"Some question the evidence of God's existence, saying all this began with a 'Big Bang' on its own, instead of being created by a loving God. I ask you all – would you prefer to equate your existence to an explosion? Or instead to look at yourselves as the most beautiful creation of the Most Benevolent, the Most Merciful, the All-Knowing and the Most Powerful God?

"As for the other man, who recently has made himself famous by performing so-called miracles, curing the sick, bringing the dead back to life, who like me, talks about interfaith harmony and brotherhood – these acts are his gimmicks. He has done this to attract people toward him, whereas I only perform miracles to make people more focused towards the

God who gave them life. To enlighten the temporariness of this world. They are very different concepts."

*   *   *

From his underground lair, the Dajjal launched into a horrifying rage at Isa's words. At blinding speed and with ferocious strength, he destroyed everything in the vicinity except his computers and monitors. He opened his mouth impossibly wide and from it, he emitted an inhuman roar. The blackness in his mouth appeared to be a doorway to another dimension. At once, laptops and other electronic devices in the room leaped to life and hovered above him. Words appeared on the screen which stated, "Activating control modules. Rerouting all military control systems. Commence Artificial Intelligence overwrite." Lines of computer code scrolled across the computer monitors as a blood-curdling laugh sounded loud and long from the Dajjal's mouth. "It is done!" the Dajjal gleefully and wickedly shouted.

In Damascus, the tanks and armored vehicles which had been shut down, suddenly turned on, with no one at the controls. The soldiers standing nearby ran away as the tanks turned and headed in their direction. The other vehicles did the same, driving with no driver.

"It's as if they have minds of their own! How is this possible?" the soldiers asked.

The group of military choppers that had been sent back to their aircraft carriers turned and banked to the left and headed back in the direction of Syria. "Mayday! Mayday! I can't control the chopper!" one pilot shouted as he leaped from the helicopter and opened his chute as the chopper moved off.

Jets in the air experienced the same phenomenon and one by one, the pilots ejected, floating down to earth as their planes flew onward without them.

Above the city of Damascus, a fleet of drones lined up and flew at high speed in formation.

At a U.S. military base in Israel, an Information Technology Specialist looked up from his workstation to the general standing nearby. "Sir! All our drones have gone offline. We've lost all contact with our troops!"

The general was mortified. "Ask the AI what is happening!"

The Tech tapped away at his keyboard. He studied the response from the AI, then jerked his head around to the general. The panic on his face was unmistakable. "There is another AI overwriting ours! Taking control of all our systems!"

At the White House in the U.S., the president was notified that the entire U.S. military communications network had gone down overseas. "Sir, we have no eyes and ears in the Middle East where this man, claiming to be Isa, had been speaking to the world. We don't know what's going on!"

*   *   *

In Damascus, the crowd listened patiently as Isa wrapped up his message. "I have talked of peace and love. It begins with each of you. I am grateful for your attention. However, I am concerned that I have ignited the anger of those who would oppose me and there is still much work to be done. But please remember that I love you all."

With that, Isa raised his hands in a blessing over the crowd, as those in the front row hurried to kiss and hug him. He spent time talking with some of them, then quietly dismissed himself as the Imam Mahdi stayed with the people.

Security officers guarding the mosque ran from the perimeter to the top of the staircase. Fatima and Ali were loading up the camera equipment when they saw the men rush past them. Paul also saw them scramble as if being pursued.

"What is going on?" Fatima asked.

Paul saw them first – the tanks were returning, their gun turrets activated. "Look, coming up the alley. How can this be?" He pushed Fatima and Ali toward the doors of the mosque. "Hurry, go inside. I'll alert the crowd," he said urgently, dashing towards the microphone, which remained in the same spot where Isa had addressed the gathering. "Everyone, please get out of the streets. Now! Run for cover, hide where you can! Tanks are moving up the alleyways!"

His voice echoed for blocks grabbing everyone's attention. The crowd was frozen, unsure of which way to run.

Down a lone alley, Tonklin watched from his jeep as the military aircraft banked toward the mosque.

"Apparently it's back on," he said gleefully. "Let's go!"

With his men readying their weapons, the driver whipped the jeep around and accelerated. Other Glass Eye vehicles followed the jeep, the convoy kicking up dirt as they beat a hasty path toward the action.

In the sky above the defenseless crowd gathered at the mosque, jets and drones dropped missiles onto the streets. Bombs hit the pavement and sent concrete and shrapnel into the crowd. Paul saw twisted bodies blown through the air and land, breaking bones, bloodying flesh. They wore distinct types of dress, noting their faith affiliations – hijabs, tallits, kippahs, nuns' habits, priests' robes. Stars of David lay in the streets alongside crucifixes on chains. Books were burning, and Paul witnessed the Bible, the Qur'an and the Torah strewn about, pages torn.

The doors to the mosque swung open and Isa, Imam Mahdi and Jamal hurried out. Fatima and Ali followed, in shock at the scene below.

"They've returned! How did this happen?" Jamal asked, in tears.

"No, this is the work of the Dajjal! Look, there are no drivers in the tanks. He is controlling all of them! The jets, the drones, everything," Isa said. "Jamal, Fatima, Ali, please tend to the wounded if you can. Where is Paul?"

Fatima saw him running, a gun in his hand, toward a truck that had Glass Eye Global Security stamped on its side. "Paul, come back!" she shouted as loud as she could. But Paul ignored her as he gritted his teeth in anger and rage. As he got closer, he could see Tonklin in the jeep leading the vehicles. Paul became lost in his rage and paid no attention to what was happening in the streets or on the steps of the mosque behind him.

Fatima took a hurried step toward him but was stopped by the gentle words of Isa.

"It will be over soon," Isa said calmly.

The jets continued their barrage as the tanks plowed through the streets. Isa raised his right hand, and gently motioned downward. With that, the jets fired missiles into the tanks, which exploded, stopping them dead in their tracks.

Isa again raised his hand, and the jets climbed skyward. He raised a finger, made a circling motion and the jets destroyed all of the drones above. He pointed to the horizon, and the jets flew away, gone in seconds.

Paul stomped toward the Glass Eye vehicles. Raising his gun, he shot into the ground in front of Tonklin's jeep. A dozen weapons swung toward him, but he didn't care and kept going.

Tonklin quickly motioned to his men.

"Stand down! If he wanted to shoot me, I'd be dead already," he commanded.

The men complied as Paul yanked Tonklin from the jeep and slammed him into the dusty street. He pressed his cocked gun against his former employer's forehead.

"They were unarmed! They meant no harm to anyone!" he screamed, barely controlling himself.

Tonklin's security team immediately yanked their rifles up, leveling them at Paul.

"Drop it!" one of them shouted.

Paul ignored the order. At this moment he didn't care if he lived or died. But someone else did. A hand gently settled upon Paul's gun. It was Isa. He smiled and subtly shook his head "no." He slowly and gently removed the gun from Paul's hand and dropped it to the ground as though it was a dirty thing.

Isa's effect on Tonklin's men was contagious. They all spontaneously lowered their weapons as Isa helped Tonklin to his feet. Isa smiled at everyone with a casualness that was a complete contrast to what just transpired. He then turned and walked away, back toward the front of the mosque.

Paul jabbed his thumb in Isa's direction as he eyed Tonklin. "Does he seem like a terrorist to you?"

Tonklin stood there, embarrassed, with nothing to say.

On the Mediterranean Sea, a group of aircraft carriers floated offshore. The captain of one of the ships stood on deck as the jets approached. He could see that if they attempted to land at the high rate of speed they were currently flying, they'd be destroyed in an explosion. Just as he was about to run for cover, the jets dove down into the sea, enormous splashes of waves sent high into the air.

Back at the Great Mosque, Fatima, Ali, and Jamal stood a few feet away from Isa, their mouths hanging open. The power of Isa and what he did left them in a daze. They noticed the Imam and others at the bottom of the stairs caring for the injured, and they ran to join them.

Paul meandered over, his head hanging in disappointment at his outburst and nearly killing Tonklin. But one look from

Isa stripped him of his guilt and anxiety. Maybe he really is who he claims to be.

*   *   *

The Dajjal stood alone in his steel-plated room. His eyes were closed as if in a trance. Electronic equipment yet hovered above and around him. The lights flickered off and on. His eyes fluttered open, exposing a bloodied, black, bottomless pit in one eye, and an empty hole in the other. From his throat, a scream which came from the depths of the earth echoed on the walls, shaking the foundation of the mansion.

His monitors had displayed the scene unfolding in Damascus: the deaths, explosions, and chaos. At first, it pleased him greatly, until he witnessed Isa seizing command of the military vehicles and aircraft, turning them against each other until none remained.

"This fight has always been just between you and me, Allah! You chose the rules. I can only influence the affairs of mankind. Convince and persuade, but not directly interfere. But those rules cut both ways. You can't interfere directly with my plans. And you've permitted me to confront Isa directly, physically, upon his return."

An animalistic, toothy smile filled his face. "And Isa is only human. He can die like any man. So be it. We'll have it your way then."

In his crazed state, the Dajjal spun into a wild circle, his arms outstretched, and he disappeared.

CHAPTER NINETEEN

Fatima was worn out from tending to the wounded, as were Paul and Ali. Their clothes were torn and dirty, blood spattered here and there, but none seemed to mind. They were alive, when so many others were not. Fatima was crying as Isa came up and sat on the steps next to her. Despite the destruction, his clothes were as clean as if they had been freshly laundered, and he looked rested and strong. Paul and Ali held back and leaned on the doors that led into the mosque.

"Isa, couldn't you have stopped this before it happened?" Fatima asked, weeping. "What was this about?"

He put his arm around her shoulder. "Fatima, death and suffering are a part of life on Earth. Mankind chose this path. Whenever truth reveals itself in front of evil, as I did in my message today, evil proves to be worthless but still causes harm to so many. Humanity continues to be caught in this cycle of destruction because man has chosen to live divided lives. To break up into tribes and nations. This division only leads to endless problems. Love and brotherhood are always there on the table, available to all, but taken by only a few.

Sadly, it is a lesson that mankind continues to face time and time again."

Paul and Ali came over to talk with Isa. He welcomed them with a warm smile.

"Here, please sit with us," he said. "I would like to say to all of you, that we get this life once. We get the chance to lead our lives in this magnificent universe with the abilities of a human, only once. So, my friends, do not live your lives by creating the divisions of East and West in this small global village. It is indeed small when compared to the size of the vast universe. The human condition is the same everywhere…people want and need love. Allah is Love. And he truly loves each and every person. If you can help spread that message in the world, both I and the Lord will be smiling down upon you."

The clouds above turned dark, and rain began to fall. Isa smiled and stretched out his arms to the heavens. "Thank you, dear God, for the rain, for water brings life." At that, raindrops fell onto the dead and injured people who lay on the streets and on the steps. As the drops struck each person, signs of life returned to those believed dead. Health care workers and police officers who had covered up some of the bodies with sheets, were astonished as they saw movement among the dead. They helped them to get up and walked them to waiting ambulances. It was without a doubt, a miracle. A true miracle. It was beautiful and felt natural, wholesome, and right. Within thirty minutes, the streets were clear of any sign of injured persons.

Fatima, Ali, and Paul couldn't believe what was happening. They turned to Isa, but he only smiled.

"Now I need all of you to seek protection inside the mosque. This isn't over yet. The Dajjal will be here any minute."

They heeded his words and ran as quickly as they could for the front doors.

The streets were empty except for burning and smoldering tanks, most crushed and destroyed. Isa stood in front of the mosque doors and waited for the next and final confrontation. It was all part of Allah's plan. Isa's Second Coming was nearly complete.

Though the restoring rain had stopped, and bodies cleared from the streets, darker clouds rolled in, blacker than any thunderstorm. Thunder cracked in the skies above the mosque. Glass in the facility broke and fell to the ground, shattering on impact. The ground shook as the Dajjal materialized on the street. Though he appeared human in every way, the aura emanating from him was saturated in hate and horror.

Isa stood to meet his enemy…God's enemy…the people's enemy.

From inside the mosque, the Imam, Jamal, Paul, Ali, and Fatima watched the scene outside. They didn't remember that Abramov had looked so evil and ugly, his facial features twisted into a snarl, his hair dirty and matted, and his teeth as black as coal. He wore black clothing so that no light appeared to emanate from his body. Seeing what he looked like now, they knew that the Dajjal had shed the Richard Abramov identity like a snake sheds old skin. The ground in the vicinity continued to shake as concrete broke apart and dropped to the street from nearby buildings.

Around the world, weather forecasters and scientific centers reported seismic activity; it was most intense in the Syrian region. Tornados, tsunamis, and tidal waves upset the balance of the globe, and residents of the Middle East took cover where possible, until the threats had passed.

Natural disasters – whether truly natural or conducted by supernatural forces such as these – had a knack for uniting people in the common goal of survival. People set aside their ideological differences to help one another. And this was no different. Political, religious, and racial differences fell to the wayside as people came together to deal with a common threat. The world faced what appeared to be simultaneous challenges from nature, and people worked together to help and save each other.

Across the globe in the United States, the Pentagon confirmed to the president that its communications systems remained inoperable. The military branches were on high alert, but unable to communicate with each other aside from cell phones. Missile systems lay dormant, as the doors to the storage towers would not open, the hydraulic systems inoperable.

"How is this even possible?" the president of the United States asked members of his cabinet.

"We don't know, sir," the secretary of defense answered. "Our technicians and scientists are stumped by the system breakdowns we are suffering."

The president gathered his thoughts before continuing. "This is very humbling. Perhaps with all our might, we need to realize there are forces in the universe beyond our control. Something we, and most of the world, have completely lost sight of."

His Cabinet members fell silent as they let his words sink in. They knew most of the world preferred living their lives not wanting to think about the possible unknown forces that might exist. But now, in the face of their current situation, these forces could no longer be ignored. And they were helpless before them. They had no choice but to take a wait-and-see stance. Things were out of their control now.

The same conditions were found in the United Kingdom, Russia, China, and other major countries. Heads of state talked by phone, yet none had answers for the global technology malfunctions.

In New York City, power was out at the *News World* offices, and Munson took the blame for having placed the station and two of its staff dead center in the conflict taking place in the Middle East.

Oh, well, I'm probably going to be fired after airing Isa's message. Or whoever he is.

The Dajjal climbed the steps to where Isa stood. It was to be a fight to the finish, with each of them displaying their full abilities in this other-worldly showdown. They would not rely on brute strength to overpower each other, but instead employ quick-thinking wit and unleash supernatural might.

"Well, Isa, it looks like it's just you and me," the Dajjal snarled, raising up to his full height.

"It always has been, hasn't it? From the time we first met in Jerusalem when I started my ministry, to now, more than two thousand years later. Though you've led many astray, you haven't been able to destroy the world." Isa circled to the left as the Dajjal approached him from his right.

The Dajjal laughed so loud, the doors of the mosque rattled. "And what about you? Carrying the weight of expectations of all the faithful believers of the world. But I took on the load of hundreds of thousands of them over the years when they turned away from you and chose to follow me."

"The Dajjal…the Antichrist…my antithesis…but I have the power of Allah on my side." Isa smiled at the thought of the Lord in Heaven. "Who do you have… Satan? He's nothing but a destroyer, a killer. Everything he touches turns black and withers eventually. Even you, the Dajjal. Why, I see it happening already. Your cavernous eyes are black with sin and evil. Your teeth are rotted and falling out of your mouth!"

Isa leapt onto the railing next to the Dajjal, placing himself at an advantage of height over his adversary.

The Dajjal opened his mouth and breathed a plume of fire in Isa's direction, accompanied by a roar which any lion would be proud to claim.

Then they clashed in a conflict that would be incomprehensible by human minds.

From their positions at the radiant throne, the angels in Heaven observed, their voices filled with praise. The majestic

Allah, the God and Lord of the universe, gazed upon the scene with a smile. The final confrontation between good and evil was unfolding precisely as planned thousands of years ago. As the Creator, He felt immense satisfaction.

In the *News World* control room in New York City, Christopher Munson impatiently paced before a wall of blue screens. Technicians worked diligently to solve the problem.

"Still no contact with the satellites over the Middle East," a technician said to him.

Christopher sighed in frustration and leaned against the back wall next to his director.

"The strangest story in the history of mankind and the entire world misses it," Christopher complained helplessly to his director.

Outside, lightning cracked across the sky.

On the other side of the world, Jamal peeked through the open door of the mosque. A frightening funnel cloud swirled about Isa and the Dajjal obscuring his view. Oddly, the tornado had no effect on the surrounding area. The breeze blowing on Jamal's face was light and typical of this time of year in Damascus.

"What's happening? What do you see?" It was Paul asking from behind him.

"Nothing. Just a funnel cloud."

He pulled the door closed and he and Paul joined the others sitting along the wall, waiting for the outcome.

In the street, within the twister, hidden from human eyes, the fight wound down. The Dajjal, beaten and bloodied, collapsed in the street. His body was covered in erupting boils, not caused by his battle with Isa, but rather by the black hatred in his heart.

"Why don't we call this quits, Richard," Isa said, using the first name he was currently going by. "Not a bad choice of names this time…or would you rather be called 'Dajjal?' I know it's customary in this part of the world to use that term. If we were in the United States, it would be Antichrist."

The Dajjal struggled to his feet.

Isa regarded him with unexpected compassion and sadness. "It's ego that makes you think you can kill me, Dajjal. But only Allah decides these matters."

The Dajjal seethed with anger. "I answer to no name… people know me without having to address me. I infest their souls; I take over their minds. I steal from them their joy and happiness, they don't need to know my name, as long as I am winning souls away from you."

He leaped at Isa to tackle him, but his arms just closed upon empty space, and he tumbled face first into the dirt and gravel street. Rolling onto his back, he looked up into Isa's eyes as the Lord towered over him.

"You have hijacked my religion, the peoples' faith," Isa said. "You have hijacked all the world's religions, faith that lives in the hearts of people. You can continue to destroy and kill or choose another path."

Beaten and broken, the Dajjal still resisted. He staggered to his feet.

"Never!" he shouted as he moved his arms in the way he always did just before disappearing.

Nothing happened, except the funnel cloud dissipated which left both men facing each other in the empty street.

Startled, the Dajjal quickly looked around as panic rose in his dark soul. He spotted a lone military chopper sitting idly about a hundred yards away. He sprinted toward it at a speed that would be near impossible for a man of his apparent age. That is, if he were human. He scrambled aboard and fired up its engine.

Isa just stood where he was, and passively watched the chopper climb into the sky, bank to the west, and fly away.

Jamal, Fatima, Ali, and Paul wandered carefully out of the mosque; their eyes squarely fixed on the military chopper.

"Where's he going?" Paul asked.

"To a place near Tel Aviv, called the Gate of Ludd," Ali said without hesitation, and with certainty in his voice.

Jamal silently nodded agreement.

Paul was perplexed. "How do you know that?"

"It's written in the Hadith. It's where the Dajjal will be slain or captured."

"Then why would he go there?" Fatima asked. Though she had embraced her faith again, she was confused by the events.

"Maybe he doesn't know he's going there," Ali said.

Fatima looked down the street and noticed there wasn't a soul in sight.

"Where's Isa," she asked.

But no one knew the answer to that.

∗   ∗   ∗

Sometime later, the military chopper piloted by the Dajjal roared through the sky above Tel Aviv. The city appeared empty; its residents hunkered down inside as if riding out a horrifying thunderstorm.

Unexpectedly, the chopper's flight system started failing. The Dajjal struggled with the controls to keep the craft aloft, but try as he might, using all his physical and supernatural efforts, he couldn't keep the machine airborne. He gripped the controls and braced for the worst as the aircraft plummeted and slammed into the ground. The Dajjal stumbled out of the disabled helicopter. Fear nearly overwhelmed him upon seeing the surroundings.

Ruins of ancient structures adorned the area. Rows of statues with spears seemed to stare judgmentally at him, but he knew it must only be in his mind. Or was it?

He knew where he was. The Gate of Ludd, as foretold in scripture.

"No! You have tricked me!" he screamed at the sky. But he knew it wasn't true. He was the master of lies and always defaulted to that mode with every utterance. But he couldn't lie to himself. He had chosen the path he would fly. Running on instinct, he flew south simply to get away from Isa. And he flew as fast as the chopper could go. Even when warning lights lit up the cockpit, he pushed the machine harder and harder.

No, the truth of the matter was that he had brought himself here. Only he was to blame. This was written in the scriptures because Allah anticipated this error. Not because He made it happen. The Dajjal was to blame for this. All of this. Deep in his dark, loveless heart, he knew that to be true.

The Dajjal spotted Isa, about a block away. He casually walked through the ruins, approaching him.

The Dajjal quickly dug around in the damaged helicopter until he found a military grade machine gun. He whirled around and leveled the weapon at Isa as he strolled up.

There is still time to turn the tide to my favor. I will not let indecision or inaction decide my fate.

Isa stopped about twenty feet from the Dajjal and shook his head at him, as if he were a naïve child.

"You are still only human. You can die," the Dajjal said. He paused a moment, then pulled the trigger. But nothing happened. He pulled it again. Same result.

Isa looked at him with disappointment. "So, now what, Dajjal?"

"I would rather reign in Hell than to choose your way," the Dajjal snarled and spat.

"Your choice," Isa calmly said.

Isa casually glanced at a statue depicting a warrior holding a spear in a poised position. With a concrete-like cracking sound, the statue ripped free from its pedestal and fell forward.

The Dajjal jerked his head around just in time to be impaled through the chest by the statue's spear.

He fell to the street, moaning in pain. The statue tumbled off him and left a bloody, gaping hole in the Dajjal's chest.

Isa silently stood over the Dajjal's body as it started to change. The skin turned completely black with decay and began to shrink up inside the clothing. The limbs cracked and turned to dust as the skin continued to fall off the bones. In seconds, the Dajjal was nothing but a pile of dust. A southerly wind came up and blew what was left of him away. The clothing too dissolved and disappeared.

"You could have chosen a different path," Isa said solemnly with a sad shake of his head. "At any point you could have turned to Allah and asked forgiveness and would have received it immediately."

Isa lingered for a moment, then turned and walked away. Light emanated from his entire being and the sun above seemed closer to the land than it had ever been.

*   *   *

Back in New York, the production room computer screens flickered back on, and the call letters of the station appeared once more. It seemed that the disruption of their system had cleared itself.

Munson appeared on the screens of the viewers under the heading of "Breaking News."

"We are told that the worldwide interference in computer signals was caused by a virus, one that is so complex that it is heretofore unknown in the world of technology," he read from a script. "Scientists will study the incident and report their findings to the president, who has asked for deep analysis and upgrades to the nation's communications and national security network."

Munson took a deep breath and stared into the camera with trepidation before continuing with the script. This was a part he didn't want to get into.

"This virus has apparently caused the failure of all military weapons systems worldwide, leaving every nation on the planet vulnerable to potential enemies. With no way to defend themselves for the foreseeable future, all the nations are eager to come to the table with peace talks."

He slid the script away and continued with his own thoughts.

"Of course, none of this explains why all personal weapons, such as handguns and rifles, have also become inoperable."

He was about to continue but hesitated, as if uncertain on whether or not to continue. He knew what he was about to say next would sound crazy. But there was no denying it, so he just plunged forward.

"But beyond the strange events that have occurred and are still occurring, probably the most unusual are the Al-Aqsa Mosque and the Dome of the Rock."

Images of the Mosque and Dome, both intact and undamaged, popped up in a window onscreen next to Munson.

The Dome of the Rock's golden top glistened in the sun. Crowds gathered around both it and the Al-Aqsa Mosque. They stared at the structures in amazement.

"These are current images, taken today. The world witnessed their destruction on live television a mere week ago. In fact, we have video of it happening... or we did."

He let that sink in for a moment before continuing. "That footage has disappeared. Not

just from our studio, but from all our affiliates... and competitors. Every individual and news

organization that we have spoken to that either captured original footage of the destruction or

recorded it from some other source, now say that footage is missing.

"Which begs the question... did the world suffer a mass delusion, or did something otherworldly... or supernatural... or spiritual... happen? Something beyond human reasoning? Something incomprehensible?" He blinked several times as he struggled with his own belief and understanding of what he was reporting.

"I suppose we may never know," he concluded, knowing the events of today could only be understood in terms of miracles.

✳   ✳   ✳

Isa bid farewell to the Imam and Jamal, choosing to ride with Fatima, Ali, and Paul back to their hotel in Jerusalem. Since his return to Earth, most things had gone the way he had hoped, though Isa too was often surprised at the way Allah designed things to happen. For example, a stray, golden-colored kitten found its way into Isa's lap as he sat beneath a tree in prayer, before leaving Damascus. He remembered as a young boy in Jerusalem, he had wanted a pet, but his mother, Maryam, wouldn't permit it. Now, more than two thousand years later, he had found one. Rather, the kitten found him.

"She's so darling," Fatima said as Isa carried her out to the car. She snuggled her nose in the cat's fur. "What will you name her?"

Paul suggested Misty, while Ali thought of Bella.

Isa shook his head. "No, not the right ring to it."

"I know! How about Omega? After all, Isa is the Alpha, isn't that right?" Fatima said.

They all chuckled at the suggestion. However, Isa took it to heart. "You're exactly right, Fatima. I am the Alpha…and she…is now the Omega!" He kissed the kitten on the nose, and she licked his right back. Everyone laughed.

The tone turned more serious as the four of them got into the car, Isa in the front passenger seat, the kitten asleep on his lap.

"I have so enjoyed spending time with all of you," Isa said. "Each of you are God's creation, unique unto yourselves. Each with a purpose and a calling. Sometimes that is hard to discover, but life is worth the journey."

Ali turned from his place behind the wheel to ask Isa, "What will you do now?"

"I'll spend some time in Jerusalem, see how it's changed. I want to meet with pastors, Imams, and rabbis around the world for a time. That will take a couple of years."

He smiled, a radiant glow emanating from his body.

"You know, the first time I was on Earth I never left the Middle East. And although I have seen the entire world, it's never been from the vantage point of standing on the ground. It will be wonderful to visit the many cities of the world and see the beautiful sites. Mankind has often ignored the beauty in its midst. Not just the beauty of the world as created by Allah, but the beauty of the structures mankind itself has created. Hopefully now, after this turn of events, mankind will have a greater appreciation of its home...the Earth."

Isa stared out the window. "And then, when I'm ready, God will summon me home again. After all, there is an entire universe out there. One day, you will all discover its vastness. Or maybe your grandchildren will. By the way, Fatima, you will have grandchildren. Everyone we meet in life on Earth has a reason for coming into another's life. All I will say is that Paul is here for a reason. And you are here for a reason. What you two do with that...is for you to discover."

Fatima and Paul smiled warmly at each other in the back seat.

"All set? Ready for the ride to Jerusalem?" Ali asked, revving the engine.

"Yes!" the three said in unison.

Ali stepped on the gas, leaving a white, exhaust cloud trailing behind them as they headed for the Holy Land.

The End

Printed in the USA
CPSIA information can be obtained
at www.ICGtesting.com
LVHW050835190424
777811LV00002B/252